MYSTERY AT GLENNON HALL

R. A. Wallace

CONTENTS

CHAPTER ONE

September 1918

"Glennon Hall was the first building constructed for the normal school." Philomena motioned toward the entrance as they paused to take in the beauty of the grand structure before them.

Delia Markham turned toward her companion. "You are a most knowledgeable guide, Miss Bergman."

"Please. Call me Mena." She motioned to the windows above them. "Your classroom is on the third floor and is situated in the rear of this building that we now face. I thought you might like to see it."

Delia walked beside Mena toward the wide staircase that led to the front doors. The tall electric light posts at either side of the landing sat atop cement corner bases. The left base bore the words Glennon Hall. The right base displayed the date eighteen sixty.

"That was very thoughtful of you. I appreciate the tour, more than you know. I only arrived a day ago and I have been occupied with getting settled into Hazel's house."

"You've never been to the town of Glennon?" Mena sounded more than a little curious.

"No." Delia took in the beauty of the landscaping that

adorned the front of the four-story hall as they drew nearer. "Though my cousin had occasion to visit us over the years, my parents and I never had the pleasure of seeing her hometown. My mother was ill for an extended period of time. Several years, in fact."

"Consumption, you said?" Mena opened the right side of the large front door and waited for Delia to pass through before following her inside.

"Yes." An image of the tuberculosis sanatorium where her mother stayed for many long months until her death flashed in Delia's mind as she stood in the impressive entrance of Glennon Hall.

That sterile facility of her memory paled in comparison to the beauty she saw now. The high ceiling was supported with baroque columns. Electric chandeliers hung above her. The walls of the hallways were beautifully papered. Large portraits were strategically positioned along them for viewing. A grand staircase led to the floors above.

"It's lovely," Delia murmured.

Mena's smile of approval was warm. "I agree. In this building the classrooms are above stairs."

Delia's eyes were drawn to a large fireplace off to their left. There was a welcoming sitting area. She imagined the students and faculty gathering before or after some event. More benches and chairs could be seen lining the hallways leading away from them in both directions.

Mena motioned to their right. "There are several rooms on this floor used as reception areas in that direction. Many of our smaller gatherings are held here in Glennon Hall, as well as the other buildings. You should plan to spend several hours of your week in one of the many rooms available for one event or another throughout the campus. All of the faculty are expected to participate in the committees. Interacting with students between classes and after them is quite common. The faculty committee room is located down that hall."

A sound to her left caused Delia to turn. Through the open doorway in the distance she could see a massive dining hall. A young boy was pushing a laden cart into the room.

"The annex was added to the dining hall about five years ago adding seating for two hundred more and providing your cousin with a modern kitchen." Mena approached the grand staircase that led to the floors above them but stopped when she reached it. "There are two elevators in this building if you would rather."

"No." It came out quickly. Delia turned to her guide and smiled. "The stairs are fine."

Mena gathered her skirts and began the ascent. "If you don't mind me asking. It's just that I've never met a woman who…" Mena appeared at a loss for words. She continued to climb then paused for a moment at the first landing.

"Joined the service?" Delia supplied. She was surprised it had taken the other woman this long to bring it up.

"Yes." Mena glanced at Delia quickly under her lashes. "I don't mean to be intrusive. Please don't feel compelled to respond."

Delia felt herself warming to the other woman. "Not at all."

"Life at Glennon Normal School must suffer in comparison." Mena reached another floor and turned to continue up the staircase.

"I look forward to my time here, I assure you," Delia said.

"You were an amanuensis for an admiral? That must have been so very exciting."

"If hours spent at a typewriter could entice you to giddiness, yes." Delia joined in Mena's laughter.

"You did something that not many women can claim," Mena

insisted as she stopped at the door to a classroom on the third floor. "You should be proud."

Delia stepped inside. The room was filled with sturdy wooden desks, each of them large enough to accommodate an individual student. Typewriters occupied the largest share of the desktop. She counted seating for fifty. In one corner were wooden cabinets nearly as tall as the ceiling. They no doubt contained the supplies needed for her many classes. A desk for her held prominence in the front of the room. Much of the long wall behind it was covered with a chalk board.

"I hope it meets with your expectations," Mena said quietly.

Delia realized that she'd been staring for some moments in silence. "Yes. Yes, of course. Most impressive." She turned to face her guide. Mena was standing with her hands clasped together, waiting for her answer. "I'm quite taken with it."

"Excellent." Mena flashed a smile then walked over to the windows. "From here you have a view of the grounds and some of the other buildings."

Delia skirted between a row of desks and crossed the room to join her. She could see the rooftop of an impressive house set off to one side. It was surrounded by hedgerows and trees. She assumed it was to offer the inhabitants a measure of privacy. It wasn't a building Mena had shown her on the tour.

Mena followed her gaze. "That's the principal's house. It's called Glennon House, of course. The school was named after the family, as was the town." Mena pointed to the other side. "Over there you can see the Model School. It's where our student teachers practice their teaching skills under the tutelage of their own teachers. It is fitted with eight classrooms."

Delia scanned the width of the campus grounds between the principal's house and the Model School. Several more buildings could be seen in the distance. She knew they were dormitories. Mena had pointed them out earlier.

"We also have our own hospital on campus. As you can imagine, with the large number of students on campus it's quite the necessity. You can't see it from this view." Mena turned to leave the room.

"The view also lacks the most important building of all." Delia joined Mena in the hall.

"Ah, yes. I see we are of the same mind. The library is the most important establishment in any community." Mena smiled to join in with Delia's jesting.

"How long have you been the librarian here?" Delia followed Mena down the stairs.

"Oh, about a decade now." Mena stole a glance at Delia. "Might I be so bold as to guess we are of an age?"

Delia thought her kind. She guessed that Mena had not yet met thirty whereas she was now a year beyond it. "I believe you have a few years before gaining my advanced age."

Mena nodded as though to herself. "I thought as much. We aren't the only spinsters here, I assure you. We should start our own club. I daresay there is a club for just about everything else at the school."

Delia chuckled to show she took no offense as they reached another landing and turned to continue down the stairs.

Mena kept up the conversation. "Although I've never learned the art of spinning, we could make it a goal for the club. After all, we spinsters gained our titles from those who held the occupation in the past." Mena stopped and motioned at a painting that hung on the wall. "This is one of the many Glennon ancestors. There are many more such paintings found in all of the buildings."

Delia read the plaque beneath it. "He was the principal here in the eighteen sixties. Tell me about the new principal. What is he like?"

Mena continued down the stairs. "I haven't had the pleasure in many years and even then I've only seen him from a distance."

"Oh? I understood that you and he were both long-time residents of Glennon."

"Lifelong," Mena agreed. "But we moved in very different circles before he joined the service."

Delia stopped when they reached the main floor. "I don't understand. He doesn't live at the principal's house?"

"He will when he arrives. He didn't as a youth or young man. His uncle was the principal here before him. Jedidiah Glennon passed late last spring."

Delia knew it was from influenza. Her cousin Hazel had told her as much. "The new principal is the nephew?"

"Yes." Mena looked around then moved over to the fireplace where her voice wouldn't carry as much in the large hall. "I understand he hasn't arrived just as yet. His wound, you know. There was a delay with his travel plans."

"I hope for his sake that he recovers soon," Delia murmured.

"He is now expected tomorrow but we won't see him until the following day when school begins, I'm sure. I doubt he'll be here in time for church services." Mena smiled at the same young boy they'd seen earlier. He made the return trip past them now with an empty cart. He ducked his head when he saw he had their attention and continued walking. "Speaking of which, I hope to see you there. If you would like, I could wait for you near the entrance of the church?"

"That's very kind of you." Delia switched her focus from the young boy to Mena. "My cousin and I will be arriving together."

"Of course. I shall look forward to seeing you both."

CHAPTER TWO

Delia walked through the dining hall slowly. She knew Hazel was the head chef at the school. It wasn't until now that she appreciated what that meant. Like the main entrance area of the hall, the dining room also had baroque columns. The massive dining hall held seating for several hundred.

Based on her quick count of the tables and chairs, she guessed it to be something near eight hundred. To know that Hazel and the rest of the kitchen staff supplied three meals a day for many of the students on campus caused her to reevaluate the enormity of the undertaking. Although she now knew there were smaller dining rooms in a few of the dormitories, the majority of those living on campus would make their way to Glennon Hall each and every day.

After one wrong turn, she found her way to the main kitchen. Ultimately, it was Hazel's voice that led her there. Although it was the Saturday afternoon before school began, the main kitchen was not devoid of activity late in the afternoon. Delia saw Hazel in front of a large range. Around her, several other women were busy with their own assignments. Four were a little older, perhaps closer to Hazel's age. She assumed those were the assistant cooks that worked under Hazel. The others scattered about in the room were young girls. She wondered if any were students. She knew that several worked on campus.

"I'll wager Mr. Wilson would be happy to see the meal we managed to produce for the faculty dinner this evening," Hazel said to no one in particular.

Delia paused in the doorway. She didn't have to ask which Mr. Wilson Hazel meant. It was not the first time she'd heard her cousin make comments directed at the president. Although everyone wanted to support the war effort, the food shortages would strain the most inventive of cooks when feeding such large numbers of people on a daily basis. Hazel was proud of her kitchen for managing as well as it did.

"I thought the newspaper said we wouldn't have to follow the Patriot's Calendar any longer." The young girl that spoke without thinking sucked her lips in when Hazel turned a stern eye toward her.

Delia watched the girl duck her head as she applied herself anew to the vegetables in front of her. She wondered about the most recent directive outlining the expectations of those at home who needed to sacrifice in order to support the war effort. Indeed, the papers had been full of the latest news regarding the measures they were all to follow now.

"The papers also said that we'll need to continue to conserve," Hazel said over the silence that followed. "It's up to our own Food Conservation Committee to determine exactly what we'll be doing in the kitchens of Glennon Normal School."

Delia wondered at the interpretation anyone would make of the latest edict. Although some newspapers claimed over the past few days that meatless and wheatless days were to be discontinued, many were so accustomed to publishing the calendars with the daily restrictions to be followed that they'd yet to remove them from the printings.

"Done with your tour?" Hazel pulled her apron up and wiped

her hands as she turned her focus to Delia.

"I thought I should finish with a visit to your domain." Delia approached Hazel so they wouldn't have to shout across the kitchen. She knew it was impossible to have a private conversation with so many listening. "If I'm not in the way."

Hazel looked over Delia's shoulder as though expecting to see someone else.

"Miss Bergman was a most informative guide. She had to return to the library to finish preparing for the start of classes," Delia said. "She was kind enough to offer to sit with us in church tomorrow."

Hazel's eyes shifted to the others in the room. One of the women closest to the range lifted her brows. Hazel nodded once and the woman turned to take over the food preparation currently underway at the range.

"That was very kind of her," Hazel said as she moved about the room checking the work of the younger girls. Above her, dozens of pans and strainers of various sizes hung suspended from racks. Large work tables were strategically located around the room. Several oversized dishwashing machines were against one wall.

"This is all for the faculty dinner this evening?" Delia asked. She was afraid to move farther into the kitchen. She didn't want to be in anyone's way.

"The faculty gather for a special dinner here the Saturday before classes begin. In past years, the principal always attended as well but we aren't yet sure if the captain will be able to join you this evening."

Delia pressed her lips together uncertain if she should relay what Mena had told her.

Hazel narrowed her eyes at Delia. "Did you happen to hear anything?"

The others in the room stopped their work and turned to hear Delia's response.

"I understand from Miss Bergman that he has not yet arrived. The family is hoping to see him tomorrow." Delia saw several frowns form before the others turned back to their work. "I'm told his war injury is causing some problems."

Hazel nodded as though finding it a reasonable explanation for his absence. "We'll meet him soon enough. If he doesn't arrive in time for church, you'll still have the chance to see his sister and her children there in the morning."

Delia watched Hazel cross back over to the range. After speaking quietly with the women working there, Hazel returned to Delia and clasped her hands together. "You'll see that everything here is modern."

Delia didn't have to feign her appreciation as she looked around. "Most impressive."

Hazel motioned to the floor as she led Delia back to the doorway. "Everything here is cement wherever we have food stored. We don't have the worries of vermin that others might."

Delia followed Hazel to the dining hall. The young boy she'd seen earlier was moving about some of the tables.

Hazel followed her gaze. "That's Sam. He works here when he isn't in school."

Delia guessed his age to be around eleven or twelve.

"It was nice of you to stop in the kitchen." Hazel pulled her apron up as though by habit and began wiping her hands again.

Delia watched the actions of her cousin. Here in the expanse of the dining hall, Hazel's diminutive size seemed to shrink even more. Her movements appeared to stem from discomfort. "I hope I didn't interrupt. I know you must be very busy."

"It isn't that," Hazel said. She motioned toward the tables

that Sam was setting. "But you belong over here with the faculty. It won't do to be socializing with the kitchen staff. Your new colleagues might think less of you."

Delia felt her spine stiffen. "I don't believe I would care to humor such opinions."

Hazel's eyes filled with amusement. "You'll learn soon enough that there is a natural divide between the faculty and the rest of the world."

Delia remembered Mena's offer to sit with them at church. "Perhaps. But I don't believe the divide is as great as you make it out to be."

Sam crossed over to them. "I'm done, Miss Markham."

Hazel put one thin hand on Sam's shoulder and introduced him to Delia. "Miss Delia is the new typewriting teacher."

Sam dropped his eyes and mumbled a polite greeting.

"Go on, then." Hazel gently nudged the boy away. "Get your dinner before you have to start on your other chores."

Delia watched the boy move quickly away. In the distance, she heard the sound of a clock begin to chime.

"And you need to get dressed," Hazel said over her shoulder as she turned to follow Sam.

CHAPTER THREE

The final bend in the track signaled that the end of the journey was near long before the whistle sounded. It also caused the man to shift his position in the seat involuntarily. He ground his teeth at the renewed intensity of pain. Beside him, he heard Otis mutter an oath under his breath.

"I hope that's the last of it then." Otis looked out the window with interest as the town of Glennon came into view.

Wes made an effort to unclench his jaw. "It is. I don't know that we have a right to complain. We skipped some of the stops and continued right through. We made better time because of it."

"Part of the economies the administration is enforcing to help conserve coal. Like trolleys in the cities, the railways have made reductions on passenger service. No one wants a repeat of last year's shortages." Otis braced himself with his good arm as the train began to slow. "What might we look forward to next?"

"My sister will have seen to our transportation to the school." Wes was certain of it. The generals commanding the armies of the great war could take lessons in organization from Virginia.

When they stepped from the train, Wes spotted a man that he recognized though not well enough to put a name to the face. He tapped Otis on his good arm and pointed. The automobile the man lounged against could only belong to his sister.

The man in the distance doffed his hat and pushed away from the motor car to walk toward them. He introduced himself as he reached them.

"Call me Arch, sir." Arch nodded at Wesley Glennon then shook hands awkwardly with Otis who held out his left hand with a genial smile.

Wes had a vague memory of his uncle mentioning the school groundskeeper. "This is Otis, my manservant."

"Lovely town you have here." Otis eyed the car in the distance with appreciation.

Wes winced in pain as he shifted his weight.

"We just need to get you settled in the motor car, Captain." Arch waved to a porter carting more luggage in their direction. He motioned toward the car in the distance.

"I'll be fine." Wes watched the two men share a look.

"You both appear a bit worse for your wounds." Arch reached down and picked up the bag next to Wes. "I may have something to help with that."

A flash of a memory came back of his uncle extolling the virtues of a poultice the groundskeeper made for Jedidiah from the many plants grown on campus.

Wes headed for the car. "I'm sure that won't be necessary."

"I would be interested." Otis lifted his bag and followed the others. "It won't be said that I'm too stubborn to take help."

Wes muttered something unintelligible. Otis ignored him and flashed a smile at Arch as the men helped the porter transfer the luggage to the motor car.

"I see my sister's fondness for motor cars hasn't dimmed." Wes slid into the back seat of the four-door touring car.

Otis remained standing a few moments longer to examine the attractive specimen in front of him. "Six cylinder, is she?"

Arch slid into the driver's seat. "That she is. Mrs. Gray hasn't had this one long."

Arch raised his voice to be heard in the seat behind him. "Your injury paining you much, Captain?"

"It is nothing." Wes shifted trying to find a more comfortable position.

"It was the infection," Otis said as he watched the scenery they passed. "It flared up before we left. The trip didn't help."

"I'll have something for you by the end of the day," Arch offered.

"Not necessary." It was impossible to ignore the heat in his own voice.

He was certain the two in the front seat heard it as well. Wes focused on the scenery they passed but didn't miss Arch turn toward Otis and the nod Otis gave in return.

The two men in the front continued a conversation between them about the town of Glennon. A short time later, they pulled into the drive at Glennon House.

"I'll handle the luggage, sir." Arch slid from the driver's seat and opened the door behind him for Wes.

Wes climbed from the car with a sigh of relief. The old stone house covered with ivy on the left side brought back memories of his youth. He used to know every nook and cranny of the sprawling three-story structure. On his visits there as a boy, exploring them was the only amusement to be had. Though he was warned each visit that the servants' quarters on the third floor were off limits, it only served as an enticement to his younger self.

He was surprised to find his sister waiting on the veranda. It was unlike her to make any type of public display. He straightened to his full height with effort and crossed to meet her. Her embrace was hesitant.

"I'm not certain what hurts," she said as she stepped back. "Come inside. You look ready to collapse."

He wondered at the moisture he saw in her eyes before she turned away. He followed her to his uncle's sitting room. He barely recognized it.

"I see we've made changes." He sat stiffly in a large chair he didn't recognize.

She perched on a davenport across from him and took in his appearance. "Uncle Jedidiah kept the place the way his mother had it. You know it would never do."

Her banal words belied the turmoil in her eyes. He looked down at her hands. She was worrying an embroidered handkerchief in her fingers.

He softened his voice. "Ginny, it's nothing."

"You could have been killed." Virginia stood and began pacing.

"I'm sorry I wasn't here." He couldn't see her face but she stopped pacing and stiffened. "When Thomas died. I couldn't get away. I'm sorry."

"It couldn't be helped." She turned toward him, her face now composed.

"How are the children taking it?"

"It's been a year since Thomas's death. They're young." She crossed back to the davenport and perched again. "But we are not, Wesley."

He felt the tiredness seep into his soul. He knew what was coming next.

"You're back here where you belong. It's time that you forget about the past and move on with your life." The look on her face was resolute. "Time for both of us."

He felt his brows rise. "So soon, Ginny?"

"Virginia," she corrected. "It's been a year." She smoothed a nonexistent crease in her skirt. "You will take your rightful place as the principal at the school named for our family."

"Acting principal," he reminded her. He saw the flash in her eyes and repeated himself. "I'm the acting principal at Glennon Normal School. Until my wound heals."

"Then what?"

"Then I'll return to the war, if necessary," he said firmly. The shrewd look in her eyes let him know that he didn't have the upper hand in the conversation.

Her smile held a slight challenge. "Perhaps it is as well. I've been thinking. Now that Thomas is gone, perhaps I should have Thomas Junior's name changed from Gray to Glennon. It would help to ensure that the name continues."

His body pitched forward in the seat without warning in reaction to her words. It caused another stabbing pain.

A flash of concern filled her eyes. "Wesley."

He raised one hand as he took shallow breaths. When the pain was manageable again, he carefully settled back in the chair. "Ginny. It is my first day back. My first hour here in our new home. Can we not forget our family duties, just for the moment?"

"I never forget my family duties," she reminded him.

He sighed audibly. "Of course not. It explains your unhappy marriage."

"I disagree," she said without heat. "My marriage secured my future, just as our parents intended. They were very wise in that regard. It is now our responsibility to ensure the same for our children."

She watched him wince and knew it wasn't a physical pain that caused it.

"In the matter of your care, I've made arrangements," she continued. "I see you brought your own man." It wasn't a question.

"Yes. Otis Hart. He'll handle my personal needs."

"He served with you in the war?"

"He did."

"Excellent. I hired someone to handle your business needs. He has been here since Uncle Jedidiah passed to deal with the day-to-day necessities in the principal's office."

Wesley didn't try to hide the relief he felt. It was short-lived.

"I've also met someone. She is a most agreeable lady with whom you should make the effort to acquaint yourself."

He didn't bother to argue. He knew her too well.

"From all accounts, she comes from a very fine family in the west." A small frown creased her forehead at the sound of voices in the hallway.

Wes ignored her attempt at matchmaking. "The young man that you hired. He hasn't volunteered?"

"Bennie tried. His family was very happy to hear he was denied for health reasons. The hope is that situation will remain in effect even when he reaches twenty-one and is required to register for the draft." Virginia stood when the voices in the hall grew louder. The look of disapproval on her face quieted the two children as they burst into the room. "Children, come and greet your uncle."

Wesley watched the two little ones approach and tried to remember their ages. He knew Thomas was the oldest of the two by a couple of years, yet Thomas was the one who held back.

It was the girl that reached him first. He believed she was around four. She dropped into a curtsey when she reached him. Behind her, Thomas tried bowing but miscalculated the space he would need to accomplish the task. He bumped his sister from behind. She was propelled forward into her uncle.

Wes tried to catch Christine to stop her fall. The movement combined with her unexpected weight caused a fire to erupt in his wound. Both children looked at him in fear when a moan of pain escaped.

"Children! Wesley." Virginia moved toward Wes but was uncertain what to do.

Wesley straightened but couldn't entirely manage a smile. "No, no. Just an accident. It is nothing."

Otis appeared in the doorway. "Perhaps some rest before dinner?"

"Yes." Virginia corralled her children and turned to watch Wes walk slowly from the room and not without difficulty. "The children will join us after dinner for a special dessert to celebrate your homecoming."

"I shall look forward to it," Wes assured them as he paused at the door. This time, his attempt at a smile was somewhat more successful.

Otis skirted the staircase.

"Where the devil are you taking me?" Wes muttered as he followed behind him.

"I discovered that your uncle had an elevator put in." Otis waited until Wes followed him inside before working the controls. "I thought it would be easier."

"Brilliant," Wes agreed as he closed his eyes.

The pain caused by the children's jostling on top of the trip to Glennon had taken its toll. He followed Otis out of the elevator a few moments later without speaking. The thought of a comfortable bed was the impetus he needed to put one foot in front of the other down the long hallway. He entered his uncle's suite of rooms with a sigh of relief then froze. It was obvious the room had not escaped his sister's remodeling.

"Everything okay, old man?" Otis asked.

Wes stared at a burgundy and white chair near the fireplace. After several moments, he found his voice. "I want this removed. Immediately."

CHAPTER FOUR

Monday morning brought with it an unusual feeling of panic. Though Delia had grown accustomed to keeping early hours in the service, Hazel's schedule put hers to shame.

Delia woke with the sound of someone leaving the house at an impossibly early hour. She managed to regain slumber only to suffer from fitful dreams. When she finally forced herself from bed, every task she attempted was with fumbling fingers causing her to feel as though she might be late to her duties.

She knew that much of her discomfort was due to the unknown of her new position. It was the first day of classes for the new term. Technically, she would not be teaching that day or the next. The students would arrive from all over to register for their classes. Delia was expected to speak with the commercial students and help to place them in their classes.

She stood in the middle of her room and debated what she should wear. It was the first time she would meet the students and more of the faculty and staff of the school. She very much wanted to make a good impression. With a wry smile, she acknowledged to herself that she almost missed the uniform the female yeomen were required to wear. It certainly took the stress out of dressing each morning. One always knew exactly what to put on.

Her smile slipped when thoughts of her many friends from the service filled her mind. She missed Georgia, one of her very best friends. When Delia was no longer able to serve the admiral, it was Georgia she suggested as her own replacement. Perhaps they seemed to have so much in common because they were both similar in age. At thirty-one, they were at the far end of the range allowed for service.

The call from the Navy to free the men for fighting asked for women with clerical skills from eighteen to thirty-five to enlist. Having just lost her father of Bright's disease barely two years after her mother died of consumption, Delia approached the opportunity without hesitation.

Like many of her female yeomen friends, Delia was left to her own devices to find housing. For the most part, she shared an apartment with several others who served nearby. Delia wasn't long in the Navy when her advanced skills in typewriting attracted the attention of the admiral's staff. Working for the admiral often meant long hours. For convenience sake, there were times when she stayed with Admiral Hobart Jennings and his wife Euphemia. It was Euphemia she missed the most. The loss of Euphemia's wit, kindness, and incomparable intelligence left a gaping hole in Delia's heart.

It was Euphemia that solved the matter of what to wear now. Delia could hear the woman's voice in her head. When in doubt, dress in layers.

She knew that the temperature was only in the lower sixties at the moment but was predicted to climb much higher by mid-afternoon according to the newspaper. She opted for a white voile blouse with a white gabardine skirt. She added a navy blue sailor-knot tie that reminded her of the neckerchief from her uniform and a matching navy blue jacket borrowed from a walking suit.

It wasn't the uniform she'd worn in the service, but it was close enough to offer some small measure of comfort for the loss of a life she had loved. She patted the chignon at the nape of her neck to check for loose hair pins and added a modest sailor-style hat trimmed with velvet to complete her ensemble before leaving Hazel's comfortable house.

The walk to the school campus was not far. Hazel's house was adjacent to the middle of the campus. There was a walking path that led from her rear garden through the school's orchard and ultimately to the Glennon Hall kitchen gardens. Delia took a different turn when she emerged from the orchard and worked her way to the gymnasium.

She began to see students long before she reached the building. Everyone seemed to know someone. The students were all laughing and talking over each other as they caught up on their summer events. Delia stopped at the entrance and wondered where to go next.

"Delia."

She turned when she heard Mena's voice.

"Don't you look smart." Mena nodded toward the entrance to the gymnasium. "I thought you might need some introductions."

Delia's smile of gratitude was genuine. "That was very thoughtful of you. I don't know why but I didn't imagine the large mass of people that would be gathered here." She knew that the number of full-time students living at the campus totaled nearly a thousand. There were also day students who lived in town as well as students who took classes in the evening.

Mena pointed about midway down one of the long rows of tables and Delia followed her direction weaving around others as she went. She heard smatterings of conversations from the students waiting their turn to approach a table and schedule their classes. More than once, she heard reference to the newly instituted victory draft that would require even more men to register.

When they reached the table, Mena handled the introductions.

"Miss Faye King, meet Miss Delia Markham. Miss King teaches stenography." Mena nodded toward the next table over and leaned in closer to Delia. "Have you met the head of the commercial department yet?"

Delia stole a quick glance. Earl Gordon was focused on a discussion with another gentleman next to him. "I have not yet had the pleasure."

"There will be ample time," Faye said as she motioned to the next student in line. "This is one of your students, Miss Markham. Claude is a junior this year."

Delia nodded a greeting as Faye continued to speak.

"The upper classmen register for their classes first. We'll be dealing with the first and second year students tomorrow."

Mena motioned to the entrance. "Many of the students you saw standing outside are lower classmen. They're here to catch up with the gossip of their friends." She placed her hand on Delia's arm. "I should let you two get to work."

Delia smiled her thanks then her attention was drawn back to the student in front of them. Faye showed Delia several charts and walked her through the process of adding a student to a typewriting class.

"In Claude's case, he'll have a typewriting course for all three of the terms this year," Faye explained.

Delia quickly scanned the charts on the table then smiled at the young man in front of her. "It looks like you'll have a busy year ahead of you."

"It shouldn't be too bad," Claude said with an easy smile. "If

Miss King isn't overly hard on us poor stenography students."

"Glennon Normal School is renowned for the quality of its graduates. We can't have our excellent reputation besmirched for lack of stenography skills." Faye finished writing Claude's name next to his classes. "I think that does it."

Delia reached for the book list and passed it over to Claude. "See you in class."

She turned to the two young men in line behind Claude. They were engrossed in a heated discussion comparing the pitching abilities of Babe Adams and Walter Johnson.

Claude gave a parting smile to Delia and Faye before dodging around the two young men.

"Gentlemen?" Faye said loudly.

One offered a mumbled apology as he stepped closer to the table.

Faye handled the introductions. "Gentlemen, this is Miss Markham. Willie and Harry are also juniors and will be taking typewriting this year."

Delia smiled a greeting and reached for the charts. "Well, then. Let's see what we have, shall we?"

CHAPTER FIVE

Wes lowered the newspaper when Otis appeared carrying a jacket from another room in the suite.

"How is it the man is always so well informed?" Wes demanded.

"Which man might that be?" Otis carefully hung the jacket across the back of a chair.

"Admiral Hobart Jennings." Wes rustled the paper to indicate the source of his questioning.

"Ah, *that* man." Otis eyed Wes's shoes looking for scuff marks. "Rumor has it, the admiral has an enviable network of spies that rivals anything the Kaiser could boast."

Wes peered over the top of his newspaper. "Why are you fussing around like a wet hen?"

Otis leveled his gaze on the relaxed man in the easy chair reading the morning paper. "In case you've forgotten, today is your first day as the principal of this fine school."

"Acting principal," Wes muttered from behind the newspaper.

Otis ignored him. "Everyone here from the lowest employee to the most esteemed faculty member will be seeing you in that role for the first time."

"I daresay there will be several members of the board and whatnot who will make an appearance as well." Wes set the newspaper aside.

"You see my point," Otis said evenly.

"I do indeed. What do we know about these people?"

"What?"

Wes motioned to the newspaper. "We need our own network of spies here at Glennon Normal School. I nominate you for the position."

Otis glanced at the side table. A crystal decanter and glass sat on a tray.

Wes offered a wry smile. "No, I have not been into the Pennsylvania rye. I am quite serious, I assure you. If I'm to be the acting principal even for a short time, I want to know about the people that work here." He pointed at Otis. "With your unique skills, I suspect you will have no problem ascertaining the necessary information."

Otis looked interested. "You won't question how I come about the knowledge, then?"

"Within reason." Wes began to push himself up from the chair. "As long as I don't have to deal with jealous husbands or shotgun weddings." He pointed at Otis again. "And I need not tell you that all students are off limits."

Otis looked genuinely offended.

Wes's tone softened. "My apologies, old man." He motioned toward the jacket. "I can't even blame my ill mood on the fiend who shot me."

Otis lifted the jacket from the bed and held it out.

Wes turned to slip his arms in. "I must say, whatever the potion the groundskeeper concocted, my wound feels better this morning than it has for days. I do believe I actually got some sleep last night."

"I'm not surprised." Otis slid the jacket up onto Wes's shoulders then checked for wrinkles again.

"Perhaps my uncle was right about the man's abilities with poultices." Wes began buttoning the jacket.

"I doubt your uncle was in need of this particular concoction." Otis went around to Wes's front to check on his progress with the buttons.

Wes eyed him suspiciously. "Don't tell me it was eye of newt and toe of frog?"

"Hardly, though I will be sure to ask the man if he has any about, if you wish." Otis picked up the newspaper. "It was Dakin's solution. The one thing in short supply for a few hours when you most needed it at the front."

"What?" Wes turned from the mirror. "Wherever did he find that here?"

"The man mixed it himself," Otis said. "An admirable skill, wouldn't you agree?"

"Indeed." Wes shifted his assessment of the groundskeeper.

"He did, however, recommend a poultice to apply at a later date." Otis began moving toward the door at the sound of a light tapping. "I'll be sure to ask Arch to add plenty of newt and toad."

Otis swung the door open. The young man on the other side had his hands clasped together holding a derby hat. He was smartly dressed in a crisp white shirt and tie under a light gray sack suit. His brown hair was parted above his right eyebrow. Though worn short on the sides, it was longer on the top and combed back. He looked momentarily tongue-tied as he shifted his gaze from Otis to Wes.

Wes stepped forward. "Can I assume you are Bennie?"

"Yes, Captain." Bennie shifted nervously on his feet.

"My manservant, Otis Hart," Wes continued smoothly. He nodded at Otis. "Bennie will take over my care until this evening. You have your orders."

"To search out the newt," Otis said amiably.

Wes offered a mock scowl before following Bennie into the hallway. "It was kind of you to come to Glennon House to collect me."

"I thought you might like a tour of the campus with the students and faculty just arriving back." Bennie stopped near the stairs and waited for an indication from Wes.

"For the moment, we'll keep to the elevator." Wes moved toward it. "If you wouldn't mind handling the controls."

"No, sir." Bennie stepped inside and eagerly took charge.

"I understand you volunteered for service." Wes didn't need to take another look at the young man's neck. The swelling was visible.

"Goiter, sir. The military doctor explained that they found a higher incidence of people in our area having it."

Wes was vaguely familiar with the term. "The goiter region."

"Near the Great Lakes," Bennie agreed as he opened the elevator door to exit. "We can see many of the students and faculty at the gymnasium."

Wes thought back to his own college days. Though he hadn't attended the normal school, he was sure the procedures were similar. "Signing up for classes."

"Exactly." Bennie sounded pleased that the new principal was familiar with the practices of the school.

"I understand you've been here since my uncle passed?" Wes

nodded at a group of female students.

They stopped talking as Wes and Bennie approached them. A spattering of laughter filled his ears after they passed them. He wondered briefly if he'd ever been that young and carefree.

"Yes, sir. I have endeavored to keep the principal's office functioning as much as my abilities allow," Bennie said.

"I am confident your ministrations were more than adequate." Wes slowed his steps when he saw the groundskeeper. The man was surveying a small plot of landscaping near the walkway that led to the gymnasium.

"Mr. Keaton."

Arch turned at the sound of his name.

Wes stopped and held out his hand. "Thank you for the first night of sound sleep I've had in many weeks."

Arch shook his hand. "I'll have a poultice ready soon to follow it. It will help ease the healing at the wound site."

The image of a newt filled Wes's mind as he began to move again. "I'll look forward to it."

As they drew closer to the gymnasium, navigation around the clusters of students became more difficult. Bennie led the way into the building where some measure of organization was in place. Students formed lines that snaked between the long rows of tables.

Bennie introduced Wes to a never-ending list of faculty and staff. Often, the young man fed Wes information about the people in advance before they reached them.

"Clean-shaven gentleman on your right. He heads the commercial department," Bennie said before they reached the table.

Wes checked the line leading to the table that registered students for the commercial department. It was long indeed. Given how efficiently the women at the table were processing the students, he couldn't attribute the number of students waiting to a lack of attention.

"Professor Earl Gordon, meet Principal Wesley Glennon," Bennie said as they stopped at the table.

"Ah, I see you made it in time for the start of classes." Professor Gordon shook hands with Wes then turned to make more introductions. "Some of the faculty in the commercial department. Misses Faye King and Delia Markham. This is Mr. George Ellis. He teaches commercial law and commercial geography for us."

Wes nodded at the man sporting a handlebar mustache and pointed Van Dyke beard then looked questioningly at the bespectacled woman who joined them at the table.

"Our librarian, Miss Philomena Bergman," Bennie supplied.

"Nice to make your acquaintance." Wes looked around the group to include everyone in his comment then shifted to allow a couple of students pass by him. "No doubt we'll be seeing a great deal of each other over the next few days." He nodded before continuing the tour with Bennie.

"Looks like a popular department," Wes commented at they moved away.

"The war has emphasized the importance of office skills," Bennie agreed.

CHAPTER SIX

Delia followed Mena into the dining hall for the midday meal and marveled again at the amount of work involved with feeding hundreds of people. The tables were all covered in fresh linens. The plates were neatly stacked at the far end of each table but the silverware was in place at each seat along with the other necessities of a meal including water glasses. There were colorful pitchers along with stacks of coffee cups at the end opposite from the plates.

Delia imagined that the placement of each item was well considered in advance and modeled after the most efficient method of serving. Even as the thought occurred to her she saw young men and women moving through the dining hall with laden carts as everyone continued to file in and take their places. The hall filled with the buzz of voices.

Mena stopped at a long table and took a seat. Delia followed suit and sat next to her as she continued to watch the activity. Above them dozens of chandeliers hung from the ceiling throughout. The light from them glinted off Mena's oval spectacles.

Rows of large columns ran down the length of the room supporting the high ceiling. She could hear snatches of conversations as students filed past them on their way to their own tables. Some continued into the annex that expanded the seating of the original dining hall. Several of the other teachers involved with the registration of classes slid into the seats around her.

It took Delia several moments to realize that she recognized some of the servers from the morning. She leaned closer to Faye to be heard. "Is that two of our students?"

Faye followed her gaze. "Willie and Harry. You met them this morning. They're the two that couldn't stop arguing."

"About baseball. Yes, I remember. They work here?"

"Several students do, yes. Not just in the dining hall, of course. And there are full-time staff working in the dining hall as well. The students assist them." Faye motioned to the other teachers sitting closest to her. "Have you met Mabelle Neff yet? She teaches domestic science."

"Many of my students work here after gaining experience in my classes," Mabelle said with a smile as she reached for her table napkin.

It reminded Delia that faculty were the exception to the rule as she reached for her own. Hazel had mentioned to her that, among other things, students were expected to bring their own table napkins to the school when they arrived for the term. Two more women took seats near them. Delia smiled a greeting.

"I know you met Harriet this morning. She teaches book-keeping." Faye motioned to the woman next to Harriet. Her uniform left no doubt of her vocation.

"I met Nurse Noble when Mena gave me a tour of the campus," Delia said.

"Please, call me Blanche. How is your first day?" Blanche shifted back in her seat as a student appeared beside her to fill her water glass.

"I can only hope I haven't signed everyone up for the wrong classes," Delia said before joining in with the laughter of the others.

Harriet leaned forward a little. "I didn't have a chance to ask you about your time in the service. It must have been so exciting."

"Speaking of which, if you need assistance with your injury please don't hesitate to stop by the hospital," Blanche said.

"It hardly bothers me at all. Really. I am quite well." Delia smiled to show she meant it.

"I still can't believe the Navy was allowed to enlist women," Harriet said.

"I believe it was because no one ever considered it might happen, so they forgot to write it into the rules saying they couldn't," Faye said.

Harriet leaned forward so she wouldn't have to shout. "Would it be rude of me to ask about your injury?"

"It was nothing." Delia made a face indicating her clumsiness. "I walked into something."

Harriet's eyes widened. "I imagine you were devasted when you had to leave the Navy for that."

More than she could ever know. Delia reached for her water glass as the student moved away with the pitcher. "I was merely a private secretary to an admiral. I spent much of my day at a typewriter. Some of my friends were radio operators or had other exciting jobs."

Harriet's enthusiasm didn't dim. "Did you have the chance to travel much?"

Traveling to new places with the admiral and his wife was one of her favorite parts of the job. "Many of the female yeomen were assigned to one place."

"But you spent some time away from home?" Harriet insisted.

"Yes. The admiral often had occasion to spend time in Washington." Delia changed the subject as Harriet drew breath for another question. "Have you been teaching here long?"

Harriet described her tenure at Glennon Normal School and her previous positions elsewhere. Delia listened to the conversation that flowed around her throughout the meal and managed to learn a little more about her new colleagues. Before long, everyone began to file out.

"Ready for whatever the afternoon has to offer?" Faye asked. "With luck, the students signing up for classes this afternoon will be eager to complete the task as quickly as possible. No doubt, they've all made plans for the evening."

Delia nodded her agreement to get back to work as she felt someone at her elbow. She turned and recognized one of the young girls from the kitchen. It took her a moment to come up with the name.

"Flo?"

A flash of surprise filled Flo's eyes. "Yes, miss. You have an excellent memory." Flo took a step closer and lowered her voice. "Miss Hazel would like to speak with you in the kitchen."

"We'll get started. You can join us when you're free," Faye said with a smile before catching up to Harriet.

Delia felt her brows pull together as she followed Flo to the kitchen. Given Hazel's pointed remarks about her place being with the faculty, she found the summons surprising. At first, she wondered at the timing. Surely, mealtime would be the most inopportune moment for Hazel to request her presence. As she neared closer to the kitchen, she realized that the actual cooking activities for the meal were complete. It was now the cleanup that commanded attention. Hazel would not partake in that.

Hazel waited for Delia at the entrance to the kitchen. She nodded her thanks to Flo as the young girl slipped past her to return to her work. Hazel motioned for Delia to follow her.

Delia did so in silence. When Hazel reached another room, she opened the door and motioned for Delia to enter first. Delia turned to face Hazel after stepping into the room and watched Hazel close the door firmly behind her.

"I can only assume something must be very wrong."

Hazel pulled her apron up and wiped her hands. "I don't know what else to do."

"You're alarming me. Are you alright? Is something wrong?" Delia watched as Hazel began to move through the room.

"This is one of the storage areas." Hazel motioned at the rows of shelves around the room. There were also cupboards along the walls. "I believe some of it is missing."

Delia was about to ask Hazel what was missing when she realized the room was filled with food supplies. "Food? You think some of the food is missing?"

Hazel nodded as she looked around the room. "I'm certain of it."

"Shouldn't you call the watchman?"

"What if it's one of the students?" Hazel's hand came up to her throat. "I don't want to get anyone into trouble. Most especially not with the new principal. Who knows what he might do?"

Delia thought of the man she'd seen in the gymnasium earlier as she examined the storeroom more closely. She wondered what his response would be to student mischief. Or worse. Perhaps they stole for profit.

"What exactly is stored here?" Delia asked.

Hazel reeled off a list of supplies moving about the large storeroom as she did. "And some of the flour is also stored here."

"Some?"

"The bakery is in a different area," Hazel explained absently. "They have a separate storage place that's closer to them. This flour is for my kitchen."

Delia looked down at some of the sacks. Although many of the labels specified wheat flour, others said barley. "The new flour restrictions," she murmured.

"What?" Hazel glanced at the flour. "Oh, yes. We're no longer asked to have wheatless meals with a fifty fifty ratio of wheat and substitution."

Delia tried to remember what the newspapers had begun to publish very recently as she glanced at the barley labels on the sacks again. "You are now allowed to use only twenty percent of the substitution cereal mixed in with the wheat?" At Hazel's nod, she continued to take a cursory inventory of the room. "There is still a shortage of sugar, is there not?" Delia knew that hotels and restaurants were required to follow stricter rules for food conservation than households. She wondered again how one would go about feeding hundreds each and every day with all of the restrictions.

"Yes, of course."

"And you're certain the thief is taking the food from here?" Delia thought it a fairly easy task to secure a single storeroom.

"What?" It took a moment for Hazel's eyes to focus on Delia. "No, of course not. There's the bakery and the fruit cellar."

"You have a fruit cellar?"

Hazel continued. "And the kitchen steward has his own storage area."

"Kitchen steward?"

"Well, of course. The kitchen steward is responsible for ensuring my kitchen is supplied with things like fresh meat already processed to meet the needs of my menu."

Multiple locations under the purview of various people made securing the food more difficult. "Where is the bakery?"

"They occupy an older part of the building." Hazel led the way out of the room. "It's a vast improvement over years past."

"The heat of the ovens," Delia said as she followed Hazel through a warren of hallways.

"Exactly. I no longer have to suffer through it." She paused at the entrance to another room.

Inside Delia could see several men working around tables with knives and saws as they butchered the meat.

"The kitchen steward," Hazel mouthed silently. She walked past the door before she began speaking again. "They have their own cold storage room to store the meat. It's attached to their work room just as mine is."

Delia followed Hazel. She smelled the bakery before they reached it.

"They make all of the breads, cakes, and pies here." Hazel paused again.

"They're missing items also?" Delia asked.

Hazel led Delia away from the bakery. "When I first approached them about it, the steward and the head baker, they both said no."

"Something happened afterward?" Delia continued to follow Hazel farther into the building.

"They both started to question themselves. They're wondering now if they aren't missing a little here and there over time. I reminded them that we've just started back with classes. There may have been a lapse in between."

Delia made the connection. "After the summer term ended and the current term began."

"Exactly. I told myself I was imagining it in the summer. Then it stopped for a time." Hazel paused again. "This is the fruit cellar. As you know, we have our own orchard here." Hazel opened the door.

Delia thought of the path she took from Hazel's house to the school. "And a sizable garden, as well. Though I've seen more than one."

"Yes, in addition to vegetable gardens, there are also herb gardens." Hazel turned to look at her as though just remembering something. "The root cellar."

"Have you checked it also?" Delia asked.

Hazel sighed loudly as she shook her head. "I don't want to get anyone into trouble. I wish all of this never happened." She backed out of the fruit cellar. "You have to understand that the food shortages caused by the war have been difficult for all of us."

"But more difficult for some than others," Delia finished as she followed Hazel out.

"Although the newspapers are saying we are no longer required to follow a schedule for meatless days, as well wheatless, the truth is that not every family can afford to eat meat every day anyway."

"You're worried someone is trying to feed their family?"

"It's very possible," Hazel said. "And very possibly it's a family from Glennon that I've known all my life. I would rather we deal with this quietly. You will help, won't you?"

"Me?" Delia felt a tremor of excitement pass through her.

It was a feeling that she had missed for far too long. The fact that she might be able to help Hazel in the process was all the more compelling. It was only fair that she should try to repay the woman for her many kindnesses. Delia would be entirely on her own in the world without Hazel.

Hazel gave her a pointed look. "I suspect you didn't spend all of your time in front of a typewriter while in the service."

Delia gave up pretending that she wasn't eager to help. "It would have to be around my teaching schedule."

"Of course. You don't want to be obvious about your queries. Who knows what might happen if this comes to the attention of the wrong people?" Hazel pulled her apron up again to wipe her hands on it. "I just hope it isn't one of the girls from my kitchen."

"You think it might be?" Delia asked.

"They're young," Hazel said. "Even if they aren't the ones taking the food, they easily could be influenced by others."

Delia thought of the many flirtations she had watched during the course of the morning while the students scheduled their classes. "With any luck, we'll know soon."

Hazel began walking back toward her kitchen. "There's also the domestic science kitchen. They have their own storage."

"Any other food sources I should know about?" Delia asked.

"Well, I have my own cold storage area attached to the kitchen, as I said. Then there are the chickens, of course."

"Who maintains all of this? The chickens, the gardens, and the orchard. I feel certain there is more I don't know about yet." Delia threw Hazel a glance as they walked down another hallway. "It seems quite the undertaking."

"Arch oversees it all. Arch Keaton. He's the groundskeeper here. The students help, of course. It's part of their instruction to learn how to manage households so they can teach their own students."

"I must say that I find it most impressive that you provide

meals for so many with all of the restrictions the war has placed on us," Delia said.

"It can be a battle. It isn't just Mr. Wilson and his friends in Washington that make up the rules," Hazel said as she turned a corner.

"What do you mean?"

"There's a group on campus that is constantly giving me recommendations about conserving food as well." Hazel shook her head. "Most of them have no idea what it takes to manage a kitchen."

"A group of faculty and staff?" Delia guessed.

"I'm all for supporting the boys at the front," Hazel said. "But if the Food Conservation Committee had their way, I'd be working with far less than what I have been. I wouldn't be surprised if they weren't stealing the food just so I don't serve it."

CHAPTER SEVEN

Faye's prediction that the rest of the upperclassmen would be eager to complete their registration proved true. Though Delia enjoyed having the chance to meet some of her new students and spend time with her new colleagues from the commercial department, she was relieved when the last of her students was signed up for the day.

"We'll be back at it again tomorrow," Faye said as they followed other faculty from the gymnasium.

"Perhaps I won't hold you up as much tomorrow by asking so many questions." Delia noted that the faculty appeared to look forward to their evening as much as the students. There was a comparable display of chatter and laughter as they found their way out into the sunshine.

"You caught on to the system more quickly than most," Faye protested. "I imagine you are quite accustomed to interacting with large numbers of people."

An image of a large group of female yeomen as they marched and were put through various drills flashed through her mind.

"Your expert tutelage today facilitated the process," Delia assured her.

"Are you ladies headed home?" Mabelle Neff joined them as they walked across the campus away from the gymnasium.

Delia didn't hesitate to take advantage of the moment. "I was thinking I might explore my new surroundings a bit more. I haven't had the pleasure of seeing your classroom as yet."

"We can correct that oversight together," Mabelle said. "I am very proud of my domestic science kitchen."

"I will leave you ladies to it," Faye said with a wave.

Delia thought back to her conversation with Hazel. "Your classroom is in Glennon Hall?"

"It is. As I mentioned earlier, many of my students have assisted in the dining hall over the years." Mabelle slowed and pointed to another path. "We can get there more quickly this way."

Delia tried to draw a picture in her mind where the trail would take them. "This leads us to the west side of the hall?"

"I see you have an impressive grasp of direction." Mabelle nodded to a group of students as they passed by.

"I have had some very helpful guides to assist with learning my way about," Delia said. "What other classes do you teach?"

"In addition to the various cookery classes, I also teach household management."

Delia suspected such a course would cover the topics of food supplies and their maintenance. She wondered how to ask Mabelle if any of her supplies were missing.

"A very important topic with the food restrictions we've all been supporting for the war effort," Delia said.

"If you are interested in food conservation, you should stop by at our next meeting."

"Meeting?" Delia smiled as though unaware of the committee.

"We have a Food Conservation Committee. Faculty are welcome to join. We are all expected to sit on committees," Mabelle said.

"Yes, so I've been told. When is the next meeting?"

Mabelle stopped to open the side entrance door to Glennon Hall. "Tomorrow evening. It's not a large group, but you would have the chance to meet more people and learn about our committee. It is one of the small ways I try to support the war effort."

"A very worthy cause," Delia murmured.

"I also enjoy the time I spend with the students sewing articles for the soldiers," Mabelle said.

Delia followed Mabelle to the domestic science kitchen and watched her open the door without unlocking it. When she stepped inside, the room she saw reminded her of a smaller version of Hazel's work kitchen. There was a door leading to a cold storage area. Another door led to a room that she assumed held the nonperishables. Neither door had locks.

"Most impressive," Delia said. "I imagine the room is very hectic when classes are in session. However do you manage it all?"

Mabelle surveyed her domain with a practiced eye. "Efficiency is key."

Delia contemplated asking about keys. She wondered how often they were used and who had access to them. She opted to play her cards a little closer. "We didn't pass any students in the hallway just now."

"Students aren't permitted in the domestic science kitchen unless they are scheduled for class," Mabelle said. "There are other areas that have the same restrictions."

Delia wondered how often the restrictions were enforced.

***

Wes walked with Bennie toward the library. "I spent some time in this building as a youth when I visited my uncle."

"Studying?" Bennie asked.

"Hiding out." Wes followed the younger man into the building. "At least they had comfortable seating here."

"Was Miss Bergman here then?" Bennie paused as he looked around for the woman in question.

"Not at that time, no. It was an old grouch of a man with bushy eyebrows that wiggled when he was most angry with me."

"I imagine that didn't help." Bennie waved to Mena in the far corner of the library.

"Not in the slightest. Made me laugh every time to watch the tufts of hair dancing about as he administered his sternest reprimand." Wes followed Bennie to the corner and greeted the librarian. Bennie handled the introductions.

"Your family name sounds familiar," Wes said. "Are you from Glennon?"

"Yes. I believe our paths may have crossed in our youth. It is kind of you to include the library on your tour," Mena said.

"Not at all. I have fond memories of the place," Wes said smoothly. He heard Bennie cough behind him.

Mena gave them a brief tour before they were on their way elsewhere.

"An improvement over the old grouch?" Bennie asked as he led the way to the kitchen.

"Most definitely. I doubt her face would have mottled in anger at finding a young boy sleeping on one of her chairs."

"Now that you are the principal, I daresay even the grouch wouldn't comment upon finding you."

"Acting principal," Wes said automatically.

He ignored the look of surprise the young man gave him. He saw a familiar figure in one of the gardens checking on his plants as they walked past. A young boy was with Arch but ducked behind him when he saw Wes.

"The head chef is Miss Hazel Markham," Bennie said. "She has been at the school for many years."

"Markham? Is she from the area?" Wes followed Bennie into a side entrance of Glennon Hall.

"Yes, sir. I believe so."

Wes couldn't place the name as he followed Bennie through the hall. They paused at the entrance to the kitchen and watched the activity as the women worked on the evening meal. Wes did not wish to interrupt them but the woman who appeared to be in charge turned and saw them there. He wondered at the flash of panic he thought he saw in her eyes.

Bennie took a few steps into the room. "Miss Markham. We won't intrude. I am showing Captain Glennon around the campus."

"Good to see you here, sir." Hazel Markham's smile seemed genuine.

Wes wondered if he imagined the panicked look in her eyes. "Good to be here." He listened attentively as the head chef introduced him to the others in the room.

"We won't keep you," Bennie said as he stepped from the room. "In addition to the head chef, there is also the kitchen steward and the head baker."

"Their names are?" Wes asked as he followed Bennie through the warren of hallways.

"Melvin Bower is the kitchen steward. Our baker is Crawford Stiles."

When they reached the room with the steward, Bennie paused in the doorway again for just a moment before stepping inside to handle the introductions. Wes spoke with each of the men around the room as they paused in their task of preparing meat for a future meal. His eyes fell on the young boy he'd seen earlier in the garden.

"This is Sam," Melvin said with a nod toward the young boy. "He helps with our conservation efforts."

Wes looked at the discarded pile at one end of a long table. He knew the animal fat would be sold and used to make soap and other necessities for the war including the all-important glycerin used in explosives. He assumed young Sam was tasked with helping to get the fat to the soap maker.

"We won't hold you up," Bennie said as he led the way from the room.

"Most impressive," Wes murmured as he followed his guide to the bakery.

CHAPTER EIGHT

By Tuesday afternoon, Delia was feeling like an old hand at scheduling students for classes. Having Faye, the stenography teacher, on one side of her and Harriet, the bookkeeping teacher, on the other side gave her the support she needed to make it through the day with the first and second year students. Toward the end of the afternoon, the trickling line finally stopped altogether.

"Well, then. I think that does it." Faye began gathering the charts together.

"Thank you both for making it seem easy." Delia added the remaining book lists to Faye's pile of charts.

"We'll be right down the hall from you if you have any questions in your classes tomorrow," Harriet said as she took half of the pile from Faye.

"Are you going our way?" Faye asked as she led the way to the exit.

Delia thought of Hazel's predicament. "Only part of the way. I have some things to see to while we have a bit of a break."

"We'll see you at the meeting tonight?" Harriet's question was accompanied with a friendly smile.

"Yes, of course." Delia stepped outside. "It looks like we might be done with the rain for now."

"I won't complain about this weather," Faye said as they followed the walkway toward Glennon Hall. "I would be happy to have temperatures in the seventies every day of the year."

Delia nodded her agreement as she considered her options. She needed to learn more about the food storage. It was the best way to determine how it was being taken. Hazel was able to provide only the barest amount of detail. She needed to get to the source. When they neared the gardens, she separated from the others with a promise to see them later.

It took several minutes for Delia to find the groundskeeper. He was working near a small white building with a lot of glass windows. She assumed it was used as a greenhouse. He saw her coming and straightened from his task as she neared him.

"Mr. Keaton? I'm Delia Markham." Delia offered her best smile. "I was hoping to ask you some questions, if I may."

"This is about your cousin's suspicions?"

His face had a lived-in look. Deep lines bracketed his mouth and forehead. More lines angled down from the corners of his wary blue eyes. He reached up and adjusted his soft, small-brimmed work cap before allowing it to settle back on his head. Delia caught a glimpse of faded red hair showing signs of gray.

"You do not seem surprised to see me. Can I assume Hazel has spoken with you?" Delia took a step closer.

He seemed to study her a moment before answering. "She did."

Delia hoped he would say more. When he didn't, she continued. "Hazel showed me where the kitchen steward works and the bakery, as well as the fruit cellar. With everyone working, I wasn't able to examine the cold storage rooms."

Arch continued to watch her with wary eyes.

"From what I was able to see, the rooms aren't locked," Delia said.

"There's never been a problem before," he said.

"What about in the evenings? Hazel is home then."

Arch nodded his agreement, but the wary look was still in his eyes. "The kitchen shuts down after dinner. No one should be in the area after that."

"I understand the students aren't permitted near the kitchen or any of the storage rooms, but I haven't seen anything in place that would stop them from doing so."

"The night watchmen patrol the grounds at night," Arch pointed out.

"How many night watchmen are there?" Delia thought of multiple buildings across extensive grounds.

"Two, though they don't both work together every night."

Delia shook her head. There was no way two men could be everywhere at once. If only one watchman was scheduled, the ability to monitor at the necessary level was even less. There could be people all over the campus throughout the night. With the proper care, they could easily avoid being seen. She was quite certain of that. She'd gone unnoticed in the dark more times than she could remember.

**

Delia stopped outside of the faculty committee room for just a moment to collect her thoughts. When she stepped inside, she saw a handful of people seated in a comfortable grouping of chairs. The rest of the room contained tables that would allow larger groups to work together. There were desks and chairs scattered about for smaller groups. Delia approached the others.

"There she is." Mabelle motioned to an empty chair next to

her. "Has everyone met Miss Delia Markham?"

Delia took her seat as Mabelle handled the introductions.

"Wine?" Mabelle reached for a decanter from the table in front of them. A cheese and cracker tray sat next to it.

Delia thought of the departmental meeting she needed to attend next. "Thank you, no."

As Mabelle gave a summary of the role of the Food Conservation Committee, Delia surreptitiously studied the others around her.

She knew that Mabelle was the domestic science instructor. Jacob Ackerman was introduced as a mathematics teacher. Mrs. Alma St. Clair was head matron of the dormitories. Arthur Hildebrand handled the subjects of agriculture and botany.

"Some of our committee members were unable to make it this evening because of departmental meetings," Mabelle explained. "We were just discussing Mr. Hoover's new initiative for Victory Bread."

Delia had made it a point to read up on the new rules before attending. She knew Mabelle referred to the mixing of eighty percent wheat flour with twenty percent substitute put forth by the head of the Food Administration, Herbert Hoover. It was the same thing she'd discussed with Hazel.

"The debate we have before us now, is whether we should continue to follow the conservation methods for wheat and meat," Professor Hildebrand said.

No study was necessary beforehand to understand his meaning. Although the country didn't technically suffer from rationing, everyone was familiar with the recommended schedule for wheatless and meatless meals and days. Everything that could be saved was sent to the allies in support of the war. She listened to the debate that ensued. It often became heated, no doubt aided by the amount of wine some of them consumed during the discussion.

At the soonest possible moment, she excused herself from the meeting. She didn't believe any of the members were responsible for stealing the missing food from the many storage areas of Glennon Hall. Delia left the meeting room and walked toward the main entrance of Glennon Hall. When she stepped outside for air, she found several students that she recognized crossing in front of the building.

"Miss Markham."

Delia turned toward the voice. The group of students were some of the ones she had scheduled for typewriting classes.

"Claude. Hello, everyone. Are you on your way to a meeting?" Delia asked.

"There's quite a lot going on," he said. "At the beginning of the term, there are the societies we need to join and the election of officers for the different departments." He motioned to the people around him. "You remember Gladys and Rose?"

"From scheduling their classes today, yes." The two girls were second year students.

"And Willie and Harry," Claude continued.

Delia nodded a greeting.

"We should be going," Gladys said with an apologetic smile.

"Yes, wouldn't do to be late," Claude agreed.

Delia watched them move away before turning back to the entrance. She had her own meeting to get to. This one was being held in yet another meeting room on the first floor. She quickly found her way there.

In addition to Earl Gordon, there were several other faces that she recognized. Both Faye King and Harriet Beard were already in the room as was George Ellis, the man with the distinctive handlebar mustache and pointed Van Dyke beard. Given the current fashion for clean-shaven faces, George was easy to remember. Others soon joined them. This group offered tea instead of wine. Delia accepted a cup and settled in the corner of a settee next to Faye.

"It looks like everyone made it through another session of scheduling classes," Earl said as he looked around at the members of his department. "I hope everyone has had a chance to meet our newest member and welcome her. Miss Delia Markham." Earl offered a friendly smile as he motioned toward Delia.

"Everyone has been so helpful," Delia said honestly.

"Excellent," Earl turned his focus to the notes in front of him. "I am happy to say that our enrollment has continued to increase. We shall all be very busy with our classes this term."

"I noted a large number of first year students," George said. "That should cause a flurry of excitement for the first few days."

"Indeed. They'll learn the routine and get settled soon enough," Earl agreed.

"I also noticed an absence of some students," Harriet said. "Several of our young men joined the service over the summer."

Earl's smile dimmed as he nodded. "Yes, of course. We look forward to the day they might join us again to complete their studies."

"Some of the changes are internal to the department." Faye slanted a look at George.

Delia watched a red tinge appear on the few areas of his face that didn't have hair.

"You missed the party we had for George and his new bride a few weeks ago," Faye said to Delia.

Delia murmured her congratulations as an image of another engagement party flashed in her mind. One of her friends was engaged just before Delia left the Navy. The party was well attended by many of the female yeomen that Delia had come to know during her time in the service. It was one of the last happy memories she had before her injury.

"Has anyone heard about Carl Lawton?" George asked. "He was really serious about positioning himself to run a business. He was always one of my better students."

Delia suspected he was trying to change the subject. Several others offered negative responses telling George that they hadn't heard anything about the young man.

"Carl would have been a junior this year also," Faye explained to Delia. "It's very odd that he should leave the normal school without explanation."

Delia listened to the discussion led by Earl Gordon for the rest of the meeting. When everyone stood to leave, she was surprised to realize that she had enjoyed herself.

CHAPTER NINE

Delia moved quietly through the darkness of her room late at night. She navigated by touch, the small sliver of a moon further hindered by the clouds as it was offered little help through her bedroom window. The feel of the clothes she pulled on brought back memories as she stepped into each pant leg. It had been a long time since she'd pulled them on.

Though the feel of pants seemed completely foreign to her the first several times she wore them outdoors, they now offered a measure of comfort. Unlike the ribbed cotton or wool pants she wore under her skirts for warmth, the pants she pulled on now were dark in color and designed to be worn by a man in public. They allowed her to get around easily at night. She knew from her many missions completed before the incident that ended her military career that freedom of movement was far more important than modesty.

When the call for female recruits to the Navy was made, it was to free up the male clerical workers so they could join their brothers in fighting. The reality was that many of the women performed duties over and beyond that of an office worker.

Although both a winter and summer uniform for the female recruits were ultimately chosen, the initial novelty of female yeomen in uniform was met with great interest. In Delia's case, that interest was accompanied with humor. When she first reported for duty, she was assigned a man's uniform. Though it was meant as a jest, the prank proved very helpful over the months to follow.

As she slipped away from Hazel's house, she was grateful that the rain they received the night before chose not to make a return visit. She navigated the path to her destination with some difficulty. It wasn't until she reached the campus that she was able to take advantage of light from the many electric lamp posts. Even then, she had to remain within the edges of the shadows to avoid notice.

She knew there was a night watchman patrolling the grounds. She had asked the groundskeeper, Arch Keaton, for the watchmen's work schedule. Delia kept to the edges of the light cast by the lamp posts as she made her way to Glennon Hall. It was hours past the curfew. No students should be about. She paused at the edge of the orchard to listen for any noise that might be made by someone else.

Hearing none, she moved quickly just inside the shadows toward one of the herb gardens. She planned to use the many outbuildings of the groundskeeper for cover to get closer to Glennon Hall. Just as she reached one of them, she heard footsteps on a nearby path. Delia dropped down into a crouch and waited.

From her vantage point, she could see the watchman walk slowly down the path away from Glennon Hall. He was headed toward the far side of the campus where the dormitories were located. With any luck, he would spend quite some time there on patrol leaving Delia to focus on Glennon Hall. She remained where she was for several minutes after he was gone.

When she felt certain that he was safely out of range, she began moving again toward the west side of the hall. It offered the quickest access to the many kitchen food storage areas including the fruit cellar. She had nearly reached the end of the hall when she heard more footsteps.

Once again, she found cover. This time, it was in the form of bushes. She kept still and watched as a figure stole near the path. Like Delia, this person was also keeping to the shadows. She wondered if they might be her thief. Who else would have occasion to steal about in the night endeavoring to avoid the notice of the watchman?

She waited until the figure was past her then began to follow as stealthily as possible. It wouldn't do to give away her presence before discovering how the culprit was stealing the food or what he was doing with it after. She was quite certain the figure was that of a man. He moved stiffly but without hesitation, as though certain of his path.

She moved forward again, this time hampered by the presence of another garden. Not wanting to stumble through it in the dark, she had to skirt around it which took time. Delia reached another outbuilding and quietly moved to the other side trying to spot the man she was following. He was no longer anywhere in sight.

She was contemplating which direction she should search in the hope of finding him again when she heard muffled voices. She stepped back into the deep shadows of the outbuilding and waited. Two figures emerged on the path. They were coming away from Glennon Hall.

"I'm telling you, someone was there."

"Sh-h!"

Not wanting to lose them, Delia began following them soon after they went past her but these two were in a hurry. After pausing temporarily not far from the groundskeeper's outbuildings, they moved away. It was obvious that they were familiar with the campus grounds and had no doubt moved about it in the dark before. They began running.

Delia tried to keep up with them but wasn't as familiar with the campus and was hampered by the dark. She was tripped up by landscaping more times than she could count. As she neared the path that would take her back to Hazel's, she had to acknowledge to herself that the two figures were long gone. She very much doubted that she would find them again that night. She gave up the chase and turned to take the path that led away from the campus.

She slowed to a walk, pressing against the pain in her side with one hand. She hadn't run like that since before her injury. She was slowly finding her way through the orchard toward Hazel's house when she heard someone else approach. Grateful for the cover of the many fruit trees, she found the largest one near her and ducked behind it to wait, holding her breath the entire time. She was not far from the path and could easily hear the man's steps.

Unable to stop herself from looking, she peered around the tree once the footsteps were past her just as a cloud moved away from the sliver of the moon. The man wearing the soft, small-brimmed work cap walked quietly but quickly toward the campus grounds. Delia remained where she was until the orchard was once again silent except for the sounds of the night.

Several minutes ticked by. She listened to the undisturbed rhythm of the crickets. In the distance, she heard the call of a barred owl. She swatted away at the incessant buzzing of a mosquito near her ear then began walking toward Hazel's house. After slipping back inside, she was careful to lock the front door. She learned something valuable during her adventure. The campus was busy with people moving about in the dark of night. She wondered why the groundskeeper, Arch Keaton, was one of them.

CHAPTER TEN

Delia held a basket with one hand and shaded her eyes with the other from the late afternoon sun as she looked up into the pear tree. "Are you certain that branch is strong enough to hold you?"

Claude's voice held laughter. "If not, you'll be the first one to know."

Gladys and Rose approached Delia carrying a basket between them. Throughout the section of the orchard with the pears, other students in the Society Club moved about collecting fruit from trees. Some, like Claude, were up in the trees. Others, like Delia, Gladys, and Rose, were collecting the fruit as it was picked and transferring it to carts. The head groundskeeper was overseeing the transfer of the fruit from the orchard to Glennon Hall for storage.

"At least there's some shade," Rose said as she set her end of the basket down. She immediately reached up to secure stray strands of hair that had escaped from their confinement. She wore her hair pulled back in one of the popular large bows at the top of her head.

"It beats sitting in class." Gladys tilted her head and brushed away the bits of leaves and twigs trapped in her hair. When she straightened, she had a guilty look on her face. "Sorry, Miss Markham."

Delia smiled as she reached up to take another pear from Claude. "Perfectly understandable. Besides, we finished our classes for the day. We're entitled to enjoy some of this fine weather."

"Among other things." Rose flashed a grin before biting into a pear.

"Hey, no fair eating the harvest." The branches above them shook as Claude repositioned himself.

Delia watched him stretch his arm out hoping to reach more fruit just out of reach. "I think we might have to let the rest of it near you go."

Gladys shielded her eyes and peered up. "If you shake the tree, we could try to catch whatever falls."

Claude continued to reach for the fruit. "If you miss, the pears will bruise."

"I'll eat around the bruises," Rose said with a grin.

Delia shifted her focus to Rose just as the tree above them shuddered violently.

"Ouch!" The tree above them stilled as Claude held his hand.

"What happened?" Delia tried to see through the branches.

The branches began shifting as Claude worked his way down. "I think I was stung by a yellow jacket."

"They love pears almost as much as Rose does." Gladys examined Claude's hand when he reached the ground. "Are you sure it isn't a scratch?"

"I should hope not," Claude said. "That wouldn't be very brave of me to surrender my duties for a mere scratch."

"Let me look." Delia joined Gladys in her examination. "You might want to have Nurse Noble clean it."

"I can hardly see the nurse for a mere scratch when others are fighting a war." Claude pulled his hand back to examine it more closely.

"At least you didn't fall out of the tree like Carl Lawton did last year," Gladys pointed out.

Rose turned from watching others as they collected fruit from nearby trees. "Maybe that's where Carl went? Perhaps he volunteered?"

Delia tried to remember why the name sounded familiar as she bent to retrieve some of the pears that had fallen in Claude's haste to get to the ground.

"He should be a junior this year, like Claude," Gladys explained as she gently rolled a pear with her foot before retrieving it.

Delia was doing the same thing to check for yellow jackets. "He's the one who didn't let the school know why he didn't return?"

"I can't imagine him joining the service," Claude said as he lifted the basket the two girls used to carry the pears to the cart.

"Why ever not? A lot of boys under the age of twenty-one were volunteering before the new man-power bill lowered the age to eighteen on Saturday." Rose reached for the empty basket when Claude finished emptying it into the cart. "That means you will need to register now also."

"Mid-month," Claude agreed. "But the thing is, I remember Carl telling me about an argument that he had with his father."

"About the man-power bill?" Rose set the basket near Delia and Gladys.

"No, about joining the service." Claude pulled a branch down so he could reach the pears at the tip of it.

"His father didn't want him to go?" Gladys guessed as she crossed over to help Claude.

"No, it was Carl. He said he didn't want to leave." Claude reached for another branch.

Rose eyed another tasty pear. "Miss Markham. Would you return to the service if you could?"

Delia bent to retrieve more pears. "Now I have a duty of another sort."

Gladys laughed. "If Miss Markham left, there wouldn't be anyone to torment us with timed examinations on the typewriter."

Delia straightened and chuckled at the look of shocked surprise on Rose's face at the comment Gladys made. "Exactly so."

***

Wes began loosening his tie as soon as he reached his suite. He found Otis waiting for him with a glass of Pennsylvania rye in his hand.

"Good man." Wes took the glass without pausing his steps. When he reached a comfortable chair, he sank into it and took his first sip. "I missed this when we were fighting."

"Not much Pennsylvania rye at the front," Otis agreed.

Wes tugged on his tie until he pulled it loose from his neck. "What have you been up to while I slaved away as the acting principal?"

Otis took the tie from Wes's hand. "I made some headway with your request to learn about your faculty and staff."

"I'm listening."

Otis disappeared into the other room. When he returned, the tie was gone. "Let's see. We'll start with the staff. Many of them are local to the area."

"Makes sense."

Otis stopped at the decanter and poured another drink before taking a seat across from Wes. "Your chef, Hazel Markham, did receive some training on the east coast."

"Interesting."

"Based on all accounts, she's highly qualified for the job she holds." Otis took a long sip of his drink before continuing. "The head baker, Crawford Stiles, comes from a long line of bakers. His father owned a business in a nearby town many years ago. Crawford relocated to this area at a young age when he met his wife. Her family is from here."

"I've spoken to the kitchen steward a few times," Wes said. "He seems like a good man."

"Melvin Bower," Otis said with a nod. "My sources agree with you."

Wes eyed Otis over the rim of his glass before taking another drink. "Your sources."

Otis gave an enigmatic smile. "There are four cooks who work under Miss Markham in the kitchen."

"I take it they are very knowledgeable about the rest of the staff," Wes said dryly.

"I am confident their many skills will prove useful over time." Otis changed the subject. "As you know from personal experience, your head groundskeeper is quite skilled. Arch Keaton. Short for Archibald."

"Quite so," Wes agreed. "I swear even the hideous poultice he left with you has helped."

Otis pointed to his own injured shoulder with his glass of whiskey. "I swear I have a little more use of my arm."

Wes examined the remaining liquid in his glass. "I wonder if the man can conjure up whiskey?"

"That would be a useful skill indeed," Otis agreed. "Your faculty are a mix of locals and others who have made Glennon their home because of the school."

"The librarian?" Wes tried to remember her name. "Miss Bergman?"

"Philomena Bergman. I understand she prefers Mena," Otis said. "She is from Glennon originally. Did you not know her as a youth?"

Wes gave a half shrug. "Doubtful. As you know, I was sent away for school as a boy."

"Your mother wanted you to follow the footsteps of the men in her side of the family," Otis said. It was a subject they had discussed often.

"What of the commercial department?" Wes asked. "I met with Earl Gordon earlier this afternoon. He seemed able enough."

"It is a popular department," Otis said. "The war saw to that. Between the available office positions and the war effort, there is no shortage of students."

"Earl was saying that even their evening student population has doubled." Wes set his empty glass down.

"There are several faculty in the department. Most have been here for many years."

"Most?"

Otis took the last sip of his whiskey. "There is one new teacher. A Miss Markham."

"Is she any relation to the chef?"

"I'm told they are cousins."

"Indeed?" Wes saw the humor in the other man's eyes. "What aren't you telling me?"

"My sources say Miss Markham was in the service."

"Impossible. Don't tell me she was one of the yeomanettes?"

Otis pointed at Wes with his empty glass. "The Navy prefers you not use that title."

Wes made a noise.

Otis ignored it. "Remember that they freed up a lot of our boys to fight with us."

"True." Wes looked longingly at the decanter across the room. "What made her leave early?"

"The service?" Otis set his empty glass down. "I'm told there was some sort of injury."

Wes shifted his focus from the whiskey to Otis. "Really? What kind of injury?"

"No one here seems to know."

"No doubt you were very thorough with your questioning," Wes said.

"Very," Otis agreed with a satisfied smile.

"See if you can find out. Maybe some of your old contacts still in the service?" Wes thought for a moment. "Who is the young boy I keep seeing about? I've seen him in the kitchen, working with the steward, and working with the groundskeeper."

"That's Sam. He works here. I'm told he doesn't have anywhere else to go." Otis stood and collected the empty glasses.

"He seems young. Shouldn't he be in school?"

"He attends the Model School on campus during the day," Otis agreed. "You should be getting ready for dinner with your sister."

Wes pushed himself out of the chair. "Let me know when you hear back about our yeomanette."

"Female yeoman." Otis ignored Wes's laughter as he passed into the next room.

CHAPTER ELEVEN

Delia followed Faye and Harriet into the dining hall for the late afternoon meal. Though many of the faculty returned home in the town of Glennon at the end of the school day, those who lived on campus used the dining hall for all of their meals. For now, Delia found it more convenient to join them.

"How are your classes coming along?" Faye asked Delia.

Delia took a seat between the two women and turned to answer her colleague. "I'm starting to know the students' names better."

"By the end of the school year, some will be more difficult to forget than others," Harriet said with a mischievous grin. "For my part, I'm just trying to make it to the weekend. The end of the school year is much too far away."

"It sounds like someone has plans," Faye said as a student worker stopped next to her to fill her water glass.

"Nothing of any great excitement." Harriet slanted her eyes to the table next to them as she lifted her water glass. "I see the motoring restrictions on Sunday are to be enforced."

Faye's eyes followed Harriet's. "Someone will miss their parades around town."

Delia lifted her brows in question.

Harriet leaned closer. "It's all I heard in my classes today. Some of the students like to dress in their finest and drive around in their motor cars on Sunday for the attention. In the end, however, they all agreed it was their patriotic duty to support the war effort."

"Ah, yes. The gasoline shortage. It's for a good cause." Delia said. She sat still as someone stopped next to her to set a plate in front of Harriet. "Hello, Sam. I didn't know you were serving in the dining hall too."

The young boy in question turned a deep shade of red. "Yes, miss. One of the older boys wasn't feeling well." Sam returned to his cart to get another plate of food.

"Have you thought about going back?" Harriet asked.

The question got Delia's full attention. "Back?"

"To the service. Now that the president has called for more men to sign up for the draft. I imagine you must miss it horribly." Harriet waited for Delia's response.

Delia opened her mouth to respond as Sam stopped next to her with a plate of food. Sam's eyes met Delia's. A loud clatter interrupted whatever Delia was going to say.

The redness crept back into Sam's face. "Sorry, miss." He remained next to Delia and clasped his hands together.

"It's nothing, Sam. You didn't spill anything." Delia flashed a reassuring smile. "Really. No harm was done. Please don't give it another thought."

"She's right." Harriet made a show of glancing around to make her point. "No one even noticed."

"Thank you, miss." Sam returned to the empty cart and began to push it away.

"He really is a dear," Harriet said as she reached for her fork.

Delia thought so too. Especially since Harriet seemed to have forgotten her question. She made it through dinner without the subject returning to her time in the service. After dinner, Delia filed out with the others.

"I have grading to do," Faye said as she paused outside of Glennon Hall.

"That makes two of us." Harriet turned to Delia. "Are you going our way?"

"No, thanks." Delia motioned to her right. "I was planning on a walk for exercise. I will see you both tomorrow."

Delia watched her colleagues walk away from the hall for a few moments before heading toward the gardens. After her adventure in the dark the previous night, she wanted to return to the locations where she saw the others out and about.

It took her several minutes to make her way to the orchard and then follow the same route she'd taken the night before. As she walked, she thought about the others that she saw. There was the night watchman, of course. She knew it was possible he could be involved in the theft of the food. But he didn't appear to be concealing anything last night as he made his routine patrol. For now, she put the thought aside. If all other avenues of inquiry led to nothing, she would look into the watchman.

Then there was the next lone figure. She was still unsure who that might have been. She paused near the outbuilding where she first saw him. She remembered using the building for cover as she skirted around it to watch him. She followed him for a while and lost him but heard two voices next. Delia moved to where she'd heard the voices.

In the light of day, she wondered now how she managed to move around at all in the night without injury. The area she found herself in was secluded. There were hedgerows to one side acting as a windbreak. She realized that she was close to where the greenhouse was located. She walked around to see what else was there as she attempted to orient herself.

She knew she was very near where the two figures had been. She stood still for a moment trying to picture it in her mind when they paused. It was just moments before they began running. She was fairly certain that they stopped for a brief time first.

A muffled sound interrupted her thoughts. A moment later she heard whistling. She followed the sound to the other side of an outbuilding and found the groundskeeper, Arch Keaton. He was working in one of his herb gardens.

"Hello." Delia walked to the edge of the garden. "Working with mint?"

His smile didn't quite reach the blue eyes under the brim of his soft work cap. He studied her for a moment before answering. "You can smell it, can you?"

"Oh, yes. I always liked the smell of mint." She saw the cart on the other edge of the garden closest to him. "You're harvesting some of your herbs for the winter?"

"It's time," he said as he bent to snip more. "I'll dry them out and store them."

Delia wondered again what the man was doing out in the middle of the night when she saw him. Could he possibly be the one who was stealing the food? She watched as he straightened.

"Well, that should do it for now." Arch set the cuttings in his cart and lifted the handles. "Have a good evening."

"You too," Delia called after him.

She remained where she was until he was no longer in sight. When she was certain she was alone, she turned away from the herb garden and crossed over to a stone building. She could tell that it was a spring house. She doubted it was much in use at this point in time. According to Hazel, Glennon Normal School had been getting their water from the town of Glennon for several years. With the help of electricity and refrigeration, the school also no longer had to rely on the spring house to store food.

The location of the gardens near the spring house made sense. The spring supplied a water source in the form of a creek that led out of the spring house, but the stone building could also be used to store the produce from the garden. Delia walked around the perimeter of the spring house before stopping in front of the door.

She pulled the door open and stepped inside hopeful that she might have found some of Hazel's stolen food. She left the door open behind her to use the light from outside. It offered little help but at least she wasn't in total darkness.

Her hopes were dashed when she realized the spring house was empty. She stood in the cool silence for a moment as she considered what she saw the night before. The two figures had stopped at the spring house. She was certain of it now.

If they weren't dropping food off to conceal it, was it possible they were picking their stash up from a previous theft? She looked around the room as her eyes became accustomed to the darkness. A piece of paper lying on the ground near the wall caught her eye. She crossed over to pick it up but wasn't able to make out the writing in the dim light.

She slipped through the door and returned to the sunshine outside. With a jolt of excitement, she realized that she recognized the label that she held. It was the same one she'd seen in Hazel's storeroom on the sack of flour.

CHAPTER TWELVE

Delia stared at the page in front of her without seeing the words that were written on it. The cup of tea next to her was cold. Although a review of her lesson plans for the following day was needed, her mind willfully refused to remain focused on the task at hand.

Instead, she revisited her adventure the previous night trying to tease out any other clues from her memory. Anything that might aid in discovering the identity of the unknown single male out for a stroll of the campus in the middle of the night.

At this point, she was fairly certain that the two at the spring house were the culprits she sought. Although she had failed at catching them with evidence in hand, their words and actions left little doubt that their intentions weren't altogether honorable. They were most assuredly involved in something. The discovery of the label matching Hazel's flour sack convinced her of it. What she didn't know was how many others might be implicated.

"Have you found anything?" Hazel stood in the doorway to the living room. She was still wearing her hat.

"I didn't hear you come in." Delia set her lesson plans aside.

"I just returned from work." Hazel moved over to the sofa across from Delia. After taking a seat, her hands went up to her hat to remove it.

Delia noted the lines on Hazel's face. With her slight figure and boundless energy, Hazel had always appeared younger than her thirty-eight years. At the moment, she looked as though she wore the crushing weight of the world on her shoulders. "You look tired. Was it a particularly difficult day for you?"

Hazel looked away for a moment without answering. When she did respond, it was as though the words she settled upon had not been her first choice. "Have you made any progress?"

"With the theft of the food? I think so." Delia watched for Hazel's response to her words. It was slow in coming.

Hazel shifted her focus from something across the room to Delia. "You found the thieves?"

"Perhaps. I believe I have a good start, at any rate. It's possible they may be using the spring house as a temporary storage place for whatever they steal." Delia watched Hazel drop her eyes to her hands as though losing interest in the subject. "Did something happen at work today?"

"What?" Hazel's eyes came up to meet Delia's. "No. It's just the stress." She waved her hand vaguely. "I'm concerned about the theft. It's been on my mind and draws my focus from my work."

"I hope to have a resolution for your problem in the near future." Delia watched Hazel begin to worry the brim of her hat with her fingers. "You're certain there isn't anything else troubling you?"

"Of course not." Hazel's fingers moved nervously along the brim. "Not that Mr. Wilson is helping at all with my nerves. This new man-power bill. Whatever was he thinking?"

"The president?" Delia tried to follow Hazel's train of thought. "He needed to increase the number of men available for the war."

"He changed the requirements for the age," Hazel said.

"Yes. It's been lowered from twenty-one to eighteen. Or will be, with this next registration." Delia said slowly. She wondered if Hazel might be worried about the male students at the college.

"From eighteen to forty-five," Hazel pointed out.

"Hazel, your poor hat," Delia said quietly.

Hazel stood quickly. "I'm sorry. I feel a headache coming on."

"I can bring you something to your room for supper," Delia offered.

"You're very kind." Hazel's words were muffled as she left the room.

Delia picked up her cup of cold tea and brought it to the kitchen. After dumping the cold tea in the sink, she set the cup aside as she retrieved the kettle. She moved a small, delicate vase away from the faucet so she wouldn't accidentally knock it over as she filled the kettle with water. As one part of her mind wondered what might tempt Hazel to eat, the other was focused on her plans for later.

**

Though the September night was still warm by many standards, Delia donned a dark jacket to match her dark-colored pants. She hoped her outfit would both blend into the night and foil the mosquitos waiting to feast on her. After slipping quietly from the house, she made her way carefully along the path away from Hazel's house.

She was more familiar with the orchard now and used the knowledge to her advantage to navigate her way through it in the dark. When she emerged from the safety of the trees, she remained beyond the reach of the electric lamp lights lining the walkways as she moved slowly in the direction of the spring house.

She knew there were multiple locations from which food could be stolen. So far, she knew of only one place where it might temporarily be stored after the theft. Her plan was to monitor the activity of the spring house at night in the hope she might encounter the thieves.

Though grateful for the darkness that hid her from view, finding her way around the campus landscaping and other surprises waiting to trip her up was tedious. It took her much longer to reach her destination than it would have in the light of day.

The faint smell of mint alerted her that she was nearing her goal. She was about to move toward the groundskeeper's outbuilding when she heard another noise. She thought it came from the direction of the building. She moved deeper into the darkness and waited for several moments. The sound was not repeated.

She slowly skirted around the herb garden and stopped next to the outbuilding to listen for activity. She was about to move on when the sound of footsteps met her ears. She hugged the building and held her breath as someone walked along a nearby path.

She remained where she was and watched as the figure of a man followed the edge of a sidewalk just along the reach of the lamp light. Though she was unable to see his face, she knew the figure wearing the soft, small-brimmed work cap. He moved quickly through the night with purpose as though on some important mission. Within moments, he was gone from sight.

She wondered anew what his involvement might be in the theft of the food. After several more minutes of silence, she continued on toward the spring house. She was forced to rely on her hands to feel her way inside the stone building. The light from the lamp posts didn't reach the entrance. It was even darker inside. Lamenting her lack of light, she felt her way about the room searching for anything that might have been left there by the thieves. It required using her hands as she crouched close to the ground. Inch by inch, she worked her way about the space.

No matter how careful her search, her hands came up empty. Finally admitting defeat for the moment, she slipped outside and closed the door behind her as quietly as possible. She stood outside in the darkness as she contemplated her next move. Perhaps she should check out Glennon Hall? The thieves could be there even now. She knew that she would spend the rest of the night wondering if they were there if she didn't at least look.

She began to make her way slowly toward Glennon Hall. Keeping to the edge of darkness, she paused about halfway to her destination to gauge the best route around a hedgerow that blocked her current path. Just as she was about to move again, she heard someone else approach. She used the hedgerow for cover and waited for the person to come into view.

When he did, she knew immediately it was the lone figure from the night before. This time, she was determined not to lose him. After waiting for him to pass, she fell in behind him at a distance. She was aware from the many times she had walked in the area during the day that there was a fork in the path in front of him. She listened carefully to his footsteps trying to determine which direction he took.

She was surprised when he chose the route that led to Glennon House. Curiosity prodded her on as she followed the figure to a side entrance of the great house. She stood contemplating the significance long after the figure disappeared inside. Eventually, she turned and made her way back to Hazel's house.

CHAPTER THIRTEEN

Delia's mind was still muddled from sleep as she dressed for work in the morning. After a final smoothing of the Marseilles bedspread on her white enamel iron bed, she went to the kitchen to make a cup of much-needed tea. A quick check of the other bedroom along the way told her that Hazel was gone from the house. Her cousin's duties in Glennon Hall required an earlier start to the day. Delia hoped the headache from the night before didn't continue to plague Hazel throughout the day.

She filled the kettle with water before setting it on the gas cabinet range, grateful that Hazel's advanced knowledge of modern kitchens meant she wouldn't need to feed coal into a stove first. She took a match from the match box and struck it to light the burner.

While she waited for the water to boil, she crossed over to the kitchen cabinet that held the teacups. She had to shift a large white porcelain coffee mug out of her way to reach the daintily flowered cup and saucer she wanted. She wondered at Hazel's need for the mismatched, oversized mug.

She set her cup and saucer down to retrieve the loose tea. It was the sight of the tea as she measured it into the tea ball that caused her to pause. She turned to look behind her wondering if she imagined it. Slowly, she crossed the room and stood in front of the sink.

She was certain the small vase she had moved out of harm's way the night before was empty at the time. It was now filled with feverfew. Though she knew it was commonly used for headaches, she wondered where and when Hazel had procured it. She knew for a fact that Hazel never left her room before dark last evening. It would have still been dark when Hazel left for work in the morning.

She pictured a man with a soft, small-brimmed work cap in his herb garden as he harvested his mint. She remembered now that there was a nearby bed of feverfew. She had to skirt around it during her late-night travels. The whistling sound of the kettle on the range broke into her thoughts. She crossed over to take the kettle from the burner.

As she poured the hot water into the teapot, she remembered the noises she heard in the early morning hours on more than one occasion. She realized now it was the sound of a door being closed softly in the night followed by a creak of the floorboard in the hallway.

All through her classes that morning, Delia's thoughts returned to the feverfew. Though she kept up her part of the conversation with her colleagues at lunch, it was the grounds-keeper she pictured in her mind. The afternoon classes seemed to go on forever. Finally, she stepped out of her classroom for the last time that day grateful that she didn't have a committee meeting scheduled immediately after.

It was much cooler outside than it had been when she left for work in the morning. She was happy for the heavy wool cardigan over her serge suit as she crossed the campus looking for the groundskeeper.

She finally found him working near one of his herb gardens. He stopped his work and watched her approach with the same cautious look in his eyes that he always gave her. She thought that now she might better understand it.

"Mr. Keaton. If I may have a word?" She stopped next to him but took the opportunity to look around. It wouldn't do for anyone else to hear their conversation.

He sank the blade of a shovel into the ground and leaned against the handle. "About what?"

"Your nighttime activities." She watched his eyes widen momentarily just before a flush crept into his face.

"Now, missy."

Delia held up one hand. "Your relationship with Hazel is none of my business."

"On that we agree," he said with feeling. "Which means we have nothing to discuss."

"I do not concur," Delia said calmly. "I would like to know about the recent nights when you visited Hazel."

Arch looked ready to begin another argument.

Delia ignored him and continued. "Tuesday night, for example. You were walking through the orchard, were you not?"

He stared at her.

"And last night. Did you stop first at one of your many herb gardens for the feverfew?"

"How the devil would you know about the feverfew?" His voice was filled with exasperation.

"I need to know if you were in one of your outbuildings last night." She still wasn't certain that the noise she heard was made by a person. And since she saw Arch walk toward the outbuilding a few minutes later, she didn't think he could have been the one to make the noise.

"No, I was not. I picked the feverfew for Hazel late in the

afternoon when I realized she was working herself into one of her headaches. Then I had to wait until nighttime to get it to her."

His scowl told her he considered the time lapse to be partly her fault. She offered an apologetic smile. Suddenly, Hazel's concern about the new age requirements for the draft made sense. It was this man she was worried about. Though Delia guessed Arch to be somewhere around forty, that was still within the new range. The fact that he was unmarried probably put him into one of the more likely classes to be called for duty.

"I need a favor," Delia said.

His eyes narrowed at her.

"But before we get to that, we need to come to an understanding about your visits with Hazel." Delia softened her voice. "I would not wish to come between you. If my staying with Hazel is an inconvenience…"

He began shaking his head as soon as she spoke and interrupted her before she finished. "She wants you there."

Delia let out a breath. "Well, then. It seems you and I will be given the chance to know each other better. I see no reason for you to limit your visitations because of my presence." She thought of the oversized coffee mug. "It's obvious that you are accustomed to spending time there."

His face seemed to relax but there was still caution in his eyes. "And the favor?"

Delia smiled.

***

"You look pleased." Otis filled a glass with Pennsylvania rye and handed it to Wes.

"I am pleased. It appears that our background is well suited to a new chapter in the history of Glennon Normal School."

Otis filled his own glass before taking a seat across from Wes. "Indeed? The school is in need of two wounded soldiers?"

"Jest if you will, but that's exactly what they need." Wes took a sip of the whiskey.

Otis lifted his brows. "You've heard then. About the training program?"

Wes smiled. "Glennon Normal School has been chosen for one of the military school locations. Our unit will also have the additional honor of preparing some of our recruits to be officers."

"Congratulations." Otis toasted Wes with his glass. "That is very good news."

"I hope to have several of my evenings occupied giving recruitment talks," Wes said, his voice gaining enthusiasm as he continued. "I'll use the auditorium. It's conveniently located and built to accommodate large numbers of people."

"The age group," Otis said. "We're talking, what? Eighteen to twenty-one?"

"Indeed." Wes set his empty glass down. "We'll need to post advertisements in the paper. Get the word out."

"Young Bennie can see to it," Otis suggested.

A smile curved Wes's lips as he pushed himself from the chair. "I'll have him start on it right away."

CHAPTER FOURTEEN

After leaving the groundskeeper, Delia was nearing the side entrance of Glennon Hall when she saw another familiar figure. The young boy was struggling with the door. Although not tall for his age, his solid frame hinted that he was well fed. Closely cropped dark blond hair could be seen where his cap didn't cover his head. It reminded her of the cap the groundskeeper wore.

"Sam! I'll hold the door for you." Delia moved quickly to catch the door freeing Sam to lift a pail and pass through.

"Thanks, miss." Sam set his pail down and returned to the door. "There's one more."

Delia held the door to make it easier for Sam to step inside. She checked the contents of the pail as he passed by her. It was filled with scraps from the kitchen. "For the chickens?"

"Yes, miss." Sam lifted the first pail and now held one in each hand. His eyes met hers briefly just before his face began to fill with color. "Thanks."

A smile touched her lips as she watched him duck his head and move off in the direction of the chickens. She entered the building and wound her way through the halls toward the grand staircase.

Her committee meeting wasn't scheduled to begin for several more minutes, but there wasn't enough time to go anywhere else in the interim. She thought it made more sense to wait in Glennon Hall for the meeting to begin. Though other faculty and staff could be seen moving about periodically, the full-time students had left the building for the day. The night students wouldn't arrive until later. As a result, the hallway was nearly empty.

"Miss Markham?"

Delia turned toward the unfamiliar voice. "Yes?"

The young man that approached her was around the same age as the students but something about him led her to believe that he wasn't one of them. It wasn't his clothing. It was common for the male students to wear suit pants and jackets to class just as this man was. Perhaps it was his business-like movements. He stopped in front of her with a package in his hands.

"I'm Bennie Burke, private secretary to Principal Glennon. I don't believe I've had the pleasure of your acquaintance yet." Bennie offered a friendly smile.

Delia felt herself smiling back. "A pleasure to make your acquaintance, Mr. Burke. I remember seeing you now. You were on a tour. I imagine your office has been quite busy with the start of a new term and a new principal to oversee it."

"Captain Glennon is settling in nicely," Bennie said. "A Glennon has been principal at the school since it first began. I'm sure it's in their blood."

Delia didn't doubt it. Her eyes dropped to the parcel in his hands.

He seemed to remember he was holding it. "Oh, this is for you." He held it out.

Delia reached for it eagerly. It had been too long since she heard from Euphemia. "Thank you."

"I couldn't help but notice it was from Admiral Hobart Jennings. I've seen his name in the newspaper many times."

Delia wrapped her hands around the parcel. "I have the pleasure of being on friendly terms with the admiral's wife."

Bennie didn't look surprised. "The principal's office deals with hiring, as you know. I saw on your letter of application that you served with the admiral. Most impressive." He motioned toward his neck. "I tried to volunteer."

"There are many roles necessary to support the war effort. Perhaps yours was meant to be here at Glennon to assist the captain during his transition to civilian life," Delia said.

His smile seemed wistful. "I shall endeavor to remember that as more of my friends are called upon to take an active role with the new age limits."

She held the parcel up. "Thank you for the delivery."

She watched as the young man walked away then crossed over to the fireplace. There was a grouping of chairs nearby. One in particular called to her. She settled in the burgundy and white chair and opened the package.

It contained two objects. The first one made her laugh out loud with pleasure. She looked down the hall in both directions feeling somewhat guilty about her outburst but didn't see anyone about. The second object was a letter from Euphemia. She opened it and began reading.

It was as though Euphemia sat next to her at the fireplace. She could hear her friend's voice in her head as she read Euphemia's words about people they both knew. It included a mention of how Georgia was settling into her job as the admiral's new amanuensis. After offering tidbits about several others to catch Delia up on the gossip, Euphemia began writing of more serious matters.

"When I first saw the flashlight, I knew I had to send it to you. With the many challenges you undertook in the name of the admiral, I am certain that you often found yourself in need of one in the past. I hope the small gift might assist you now if some current problem requires illumination."

Delia's fingers wrapped around the flashlight. Dear, understanding Euphemia. How like her to know that Delia would be unable to resist any chance at righting a wrong, no matter how small her involvement, and that it might entail late-night activities.

The sound of a muffled curse startled her. Delia used the letter to shield the flashlight in her hand as she stood to face the speaker. Her eyes widened when she recognized the new principal. She pressed her lips together just in time, effectively stopping the reprimand on her tongue for the language he used. She wondered at the lack of color in his face as he stood glaring at her.

After several moments, Delia opted to end the tense silence. "Captain Glennon. Do you require assistance?"

His lips moved but nothing came out. When he finally found his voice, it sounded harsh. "You have me at a disadvantage. You look familiar but at the moment I cannot recall a name to match."

"Miss Delia Markham." She watched his eyes return briefly to the chair behind her. "I'm the new typewriting teacher."

"Ah, yes. The yeomanette." He turned his head to look away.

Delia felt her chin go up and reminded herself that he was her new boss. "Female yeoman, Captain."

He nodded his head once as though acknowledging the correction. When his eyes returned to hers, they held a small flicker of humor though the lines bracketing his mouth appeared more pronounced. "My apologies, Miss Markham."

She watched him look around as though searching for a way out.

He turned his focus back to her and offered a wry smile. "It seems I've managed to temporarily misplace my private secretary."

"He was here not lot ago." Delia motioned toward the main entrance. "I believe he left the building." She stood staring at the entrance long after the new principal left in search of Bennie.

CHAPTER FIFTEEN

After finishing his work with Bennie, Wes returned to his private suite to have a drink before dinner. He had just poured himself a healthy portion of Pennsylvania rye from the decanter when Otis appeared beside him and snatched the glass from his hands.

"Not tonight, old man. Sorry." Otis didn't look sorry as he sipped from the glass.

"Blighter! Get your own drink." Wes crossed back to the decanter to get another glass.

"I believe you'll be in need of all your wits for dinner this evening."

It was the warning tone of Otis's voice that gave him his first clue.

Wes groaned. "Don't tell me."

"Your sister has guests. They are in the parlor even as we speak."

Wes covered his eyes with his hand as thoughts of a quiet dinner followed by a pleasant evening spent in the privacy of his suite with more Pennsylvania rye disappeared in smoke.

"She didn't."

"From what I can tell, her lady friend has much to commend her." Otis took another drink.

Wes dropped his hand. "Well, there's nothing I can do about it now but put on a brave face. Have you picked out my clothes?"

"They await you in the dressing room." Otis took a seat.

"Don't finish the bottle before I return," Wes grumbled as he left the room.

"I wouldn't dream of it," Otis said.

Wes heard him laughing in the other room. When he finished dressing for dinner, he returned to find Otis standing near the door to the hall waiting for him. Wes paused in front of Otis to let him finish his inspection.

Otis adjusted the knot on Wes's tie. "I suppose you'll do."

"Wish me luck," Wes said as he opened the door.

"With the lady?" Otis asked.

"With a quick end to the meal," Wes said under his breath as he left the room.

He considered using the elevator to reach the first floor then opted to struggle down the stairs. He heard voices as he neared the drawing room. The sound of his sister's laughter stopped him in his tracks just outside the door. It was a natural sound, not the well-modulated tone she adopted in front of others. He wondered when he'd last heard her genuinely happy. An image of the two of them as young children came to mind.

"I wonder where my brother has gotten to. Oh, there he is. Wesley, come in here." Virginia crossed over to him and looped her arm in his. "These are the two that I mentioned to you. Mrs. Araminta Whitmer and her cousin, Mr. Chester Vanderlin."

Wes made the appropriate greetings. When Virginia freed his

arm, he stepped forward to shake hands with Chester.

"I was hoping to give them a tour of the campus after dinner," Virginia said with a lift of her brows at her brother.

"I'm afraid I am to blame for that," Araminta said with an apologetic smile. "I've never met anyone with a school named after them. It all sounds so very interesting."

"Virginia was telling us about the new military training school," Chester said as he stopped next to Virginia. He held his arm out to escort her into the dining room.

Wes was left standing next to Araminta with a bemused look on his face. Belatedly, he held his arm out. "My apologies. I wasn't aware that news was made public yet. I only just heard a few moments ago. I believe there's something my sister hasn't mentioned to me yet."

Araminta gave him an understanding smile. "I won't tell tales between siblings."

Wes was fairly certain he knew what that meant. After helping Araminta to her seat and taking his own, he addressed his sister. "Need I assume that I have you to thank for the military training school?"

"You can serve now," Virginia told the servant before turning back to Wes. "Perhaps we should save that discussion for after dinner?"

Her smile was the practiced one he was used to seeing in public. He was immediately sorry he chased the other away. He nodded his agreement and applied himself to the conversation that followed. By the time the dinner was over, he was laughing along with Virginia as he helped Araminta into her coat.

"Just a short tour," Araminta promised. "We don't want to keep you long. I know you must be worn out after spending your whole day there. We'll leave directly after seeing some of the buildings up close."

Wes walked beside her telling Araminta and Chester as much as he could remember about the school and the buildings they passed. As promised, the two visitors didn't keep the Glennon siblings much longer. At the end of the tour, he stood with his sister in front of Glennon House waving at the motor car as they drove away.

"Well, what did you think?" Virginia turned to go into the house.

Wes climbed the front steps of the veranda with her. "I must say, I don't recall the last time I laughed like that."

Virginia looked surprised, then pleased.

He opened the front door for her. "You never answered. Should I thank you for the military training school as well?"

She didn't look at him as she slid her coat off. "I may have made a phone call or two. I did it for you."

"I know that," he said quietly. "And I do thank you."

After passing her coat to a maid, she looped her arm in his and walked beside him. "I had to think of something to tempt you to stay."

He felt the smile pull at his lips. "Does that explain the lovely Mrs. Araminta Whitmer as well?"

"It is hardly a chore to suffer her presence," Virginia pointed out.

"Agreed," he said amiably as they reached the drawing room. He crossed over to a tray with a decanter and held it up. At her nod, he poured them both a drink. "A widow, I presume?"

"Of course. Like me, she lost her husband early in the war."

"And her cousin, Chester Vanderlin? He is also not a dullard."

"Hardly," she agreed as she took the glass from him. A small furrow appeared momentarily between her brows as she studied the glass in her hand. "You were right, you know. I didn't marry my husband for love. I did it because our parents wanted me to. I would do it again." Her voice held conviction. "He may have died in the war before his time, but he left me very well off when he did it. My children are cared for."

Wes didn't argue with her. "But now you're thinking you might want to try a different kind of relationship?"

"I confess, I was always a little jealous of the one you had with Barbara, before her death. Though you've never said if you were happy together. At the end, I began to wonder." Her eyes went to his. "I do not yet know if the man in question is worthy."

"But you are intrigued enough to find out?" he guessed. He saw the answer in her eyes. "Then I shall make the effort to know him better."

CHAPTER SIXTEEN

After donning her typical wardrobe to go out at night, Delia added a jacket over a dark wool sweater for warmth. As she fastened on her service boots, she wished for the soft work cap worn by the groundskeeper to complete her outfit. She stole away from the house quietly. If there was one thing she had learned over the past several outings it was that the nightlife around the campus was fairly active.

As she navigated her way slowly along the trail from Hazel's house to the school orchard, she reached into her pocket to feel the comforting form of the flashlight Euphemia had sent to her. At a little over six inches long, it fit perfectly in her pocket.

When she reached the first row of fruit trees, she blended in between a row rather than follow the main trail. As silently as possible, she continued her way closer to her destination across the grass. She knew that the thieves were taking the food from one or more of the many areas in Glennon Hall. She assumed they were temporarily storing it in the spring house until they could move it again.

Her guess was that the thieves might be living in one of the dormitories on campus. That would offer one explanation for why they needed the temporary storage area. They couldn't bring the food back to their rooms without risking exposure. Because off-campus thieves could also have need for such a storage area, she hadn't completely ruled them out as suspects.

The sound of crickets in the orchard was nearly overwhelming. She relied on it to help cover any noises she might make. After leaving the safety of the fruit trees, the din of their night songs lessened as she left many of them behind. Delia paused to listen. She could hear the sound of footsteps on the walkway. In the distance, she saw the night watchman walking away from her in the direction of the dormitories.

She turned and went the opposite direction toward the general area of Glennon Hall. She took an indirect route to get there stopping first at the spring house to listen again. Although she didn't hear anything, she sensed that she wasn't alone.

Her suspicions were confirmed when a hand reached from behind her and clamped over her mouth. A strong arm circled around her. Delia immediately folded her arm and swung the point of her elbow toward her captor.

"Ouch! What did you do that for?"

She turned to face Arch Keaton.

"Why did you sneak up on me?" she demanded as quietly as she could.

"I was afraid you would scream." He rubbed his side.

"Why would I scream? I was the one who told you to meet me here." She shook her head in the darkness. "Never mind. We need to find the thieves."

"I still say you're crazy for doing this." He stepped closer to the spring house to use it as cover.

"You are welcome to your opinion," she whispered back.

"It isn't safe for you to be about at night," he continued.

"You have my permission to leave," she hissed back.

"If something happened to you, Hazel would never forgive me."

There was that. It was something she had counted on when she asked him for the favor. "Then let's do what we need to do."

She took his silence for agreement and started to say something else. His hand on her arm stopped her. They stood side-by-side for several moments. At first, Delia couldn't hear anything above the night sounds. Then there was a soft scuffing noise. After several more moments, muffled footsteps could be heard.

Eventually, two figures emerged from the darkness. Delia hugged the spring house next to Arch and held her breath. The figures continued moving toward the direction of Glennon Hall. She waited for several moments after they passed before speaking again. When she did, she whispered her idea to Arch. He vehemently disagreed with her plan.

"I cannot force you to help me," Delia said before slipping away to follow the two figures in the night.

She kept outside the range of the lamp lights and moved as quietly as possible toward Glennon Hall. When she had the hall in view, she found cover behind some hedgerows and waited. Arch joined her a moment later. Together they watched as a light shone near the side entrance to Glennon Hall. It was as Delia had suspected. A supply truck had arrived earlier in the day to restock the many storage areas inside. The thieves were planning to take some of the new stock.

"They must have a flashlight," Arch said.

The comment gave her an idea. "Once they have the food from the storage areas, they'll need to store it in the spring house."

"Yeah. So?"

"You said you didn't want me to help you catch them," she reminded him.

"Now you're finally talking sense," he muttered.

"That means we need help." She told him her idea.

"It's an improvement over you getting into a tussle with them." He still didn't sound convinced.

She chose to accept his comment as agreement. "You go now. I'll stay and watch them."

"That's the part I don't like."

She wasn't going to argue with him. She doubted they had much time. The thieves must surely know the routine of the night watchman just as well as she did. Their window of opportunity was closing. The thieves had to make their move now.

She reached up and pushed against his arm. He took the hint. One moment he was there. The next he was gone. Delia remained where she was and watched for the slivers of light to reappear near the entrance to Glennon Hall. It seemed to take forever.

When she finally saw them, the two figures were moving more slowly and no longer looked like men. They now held bulky shapes over their backs and moved more awkwardly. She had no trouble following them back toward the spring house. They stopped often to shift their burdens in the darkness. They kept to the edge of the light as they moved.

Not wanting to be seen, she moved deeper into the darkness. It meant taking more care to avoid tripping but the slow movement of the thieves made it possible to keep pace with them. As they neared the spring house, she hoped that Arch had managed to find the night watchman. Discovering the two figures out at night in the general vicinity of the stolen goods would be cause for suspicion. Apprehending the thieves with the stolen goods was more incriminating.

Shortly before they reached the spring house, Delia positioned herself and slid the flashlight from her pocket. She switched on the flashlight aiming it toward the entrance to the spring house just as the figures reached it. The two men were illuminated in the light. Both froze in place.

She heard a man's voice shout out. "You there! Stop!"

She kept her flashlight aimed toward the two figures and waited until two more figures joined them. It didn't take long before the thieves were subdued. Delia slipped away before the night watchman had a chance to go looking for the origin of the light she held in her hand.

She was finishing a cup of tea in Hazel's kitchen a short time later when she heard a soft tapping on the door. It opened a moment later and Arch stepped inside.

"You were right. It was two of the students," he said quietly. "We questioned them pretty thoroughly. They were selling it for the money. They said they needed the income to help support their families and remain in school."

Delia wrapped her hands around the empty teacup. "I'm sorry to hear that."

"Good night, miss."

As she rinsed the teacup in the sink, Delia wondered if the news of the students stealing for necessity would make it easier or harder for Hazel to accept.

CHAPTER SEVENTEEN

Wesley lowered the newspaper and eyed the coffee pot on the sideboard across the dining room of Glennon House at breakfast. He debated getting up to refill his cup.

"It won't grow legs and come to you," Otis said from the other side of the table. He lowered his newspaper enough to peer over the top. "Would you like me to get it for you?"

"That would be uncommonly kind of you," Wes said as his newspaper went back up. He read another page before lowering it again. Otis hadn't moved. Wes set his section of the newspaper on the table and pushed himself up from his chair.

"Are you done with that?" Otis asked from behind his newspaper.

Wes snatched up his section of the newspaper and tossed it at Otis before crossing over toward the coffee on the sideboard. He stopped next to Otis first to fill his cup.

"I believe I need a new manservant," Wes said.

Otis grunted an agreement.

Wes moved to the other side of the table. "There's always that young man that works for the school."

"Sam," Otis supplied.

"Exactly. He appears to be full of energy. Something you and I obviously lack. Though I'm not certain he's entirely stable." Wes filled his cup then set the coffee down on the table and took his seat. "I saw him yesterday, late in the afternoon. He was eating his meal in between his chores."

Otis lowered his newspaper and reached for his coffee cup as he listened to Wes.

Wes dropped his eyes to the coffee cup in front of him. "I suggested that he drink a glass of milk with his food because it was good for him. The boy acted like I was trying to poison him."

"No doubt." Otis set his newspaper on the table. "His mother died of milk sickness. Lost his siblings from it also. Young Sam was sick but recovered. His father was so distraught, he left the area. No one has heard from him since. That's why the boy lives here."

"Well, that would explain it." Wes picked up his coffee cup. "I take it this tidbit was gleaned from one of the women in the kitchen?"

"They are a fountain of knowledge," Otis agreed amiably.

"In your never-ending quest to divest them of their many secrets, were you able to learn anything else about the faculty and staff here?"

"Getting to know the women here is but one of the many sacrifices I make on your behalf." Otis's face turned thoughtful. "There was something interesting about the female Yeoman Second Class of the Naval Reserve Force."

"Oh? Do tell."

"Mind you, it's only rumor." Otis checked the doorway to see if any of the servants were about. "I have yet to confirm it unconditionally."

"I trust your ability to ferret out even the best-kept secrets," Wes said.

"Perhaps not in this case," Otis warned. "I was able to gather only the smallest part of the story and it wasn't from anyone here. I had to make several phone calls to our friends in Washington even for this small morsel."

"You have my attention."

"It's regarding the incident that ended her military career."

Wes chuckled as he set his coffee cup down. "Don't tell me it was because she was tired of the uniform. Didn't like the color, eh?"

Otis put an abrupt end to Wes's amusement. "From what I've been told, the woman was stabbed with a knife."

***

Delia descended the steps from her classroom to the first floor of Glennon Hall. She was early for her committee meeting but her class had ended several minutes ago. As she reached the bottom of the grand staircase, she debated stepping outside for some fresh air.

"Miss Markham."

She turned toward the voice. A small group of students were gathered around the sitting area near the fireplace. Delia crossed over to join them.

"Have you heard?" Gladys asked.

Delia lifted her brows. "About?"

"The food thieves." Gladys looked around and took a step closer. When she spoke again, her voice was quieter but full of excitement. "We heard it was Willie and Harry."

Delia knew it was but had no intention of confirming the story now. She also didn't feel comfortable asking for any details the students may have heard but she did want to know. She hesitated long enough for the others to join the conversation.

"I heard they were selling the food for profit," Rose said.

Claude's forehead furrowed with his frown. "They deserve whatever punishment they're given."

"Haven't you heard?" Gladys looked around the hallway before speaking again. "They haven't been turned over to the police. I'm told that they needed the money for their families. Principal Glennon plans to deal with it." Her smile gave away her excitement at being the one to tell them the news.

"What do you think he'll do?" Rose asked.

"Maybe the captain will punish them like they do in the service?" Claude suggested.

"What does that mean?" Rose asked.

"It means you shouldn't be discussing this," Faye King said as she approached them from the stairs.

"Sorry, Miss King." Gladys pressed her lips together to stifle her smile but the glimmer of excitement remained in her eyes. "It's just that the principal is new to the school."

"And he is from the military," Rose added. "We aren't certain what he might do."

"Whereas I am quite certain that all of you have schoolwork to complete." Faye made eye contact with each of them.

Gladys slanted a look at Rose. "I was planning to do mine later."

Rose began moving away with the others. "I already have a start on mine."

Delia turned to Faye as the group moved away. "You can't blame them for being curious."

Faye motioned toward the furniture. "And I don't. Mind if I

wait here with you for the committee meeting?"

"Have you heard anything about the thefts?" Delia sat in the burgundy and white chair.

Faye hummed a negative response. "Only what the students said in my classes today and most of that was probably wrong."

Delia had heard her fair share of speculation as well. "What punishment might the principal apply, do you know?" She was debating if she should approach the man and speak to him about it. Though she wasn't yet able to speak with Hazel at length, she knew her cousin was concerned about the predicament of the thieves. They were two of the many students who worked with the kitchen staff to serve the food.

"I have no idea. I don't know the man. Not really." Faye smiled a greeting as Mena joined them. "Here is another committee member waiting for the meeting to begin."

Mena sat next to Faye. "Is this about the latest gossip? That's all the students have talked about in the library today."

"Delia was asking about our principal," Faye said. "And the punishment he might mete out. You know him better than the rest of us. What do you think?"

Mena's wry smile indicated her disagreement. "I cannot claim a special knowledge of the man. We grew up in the same town, of course. I know *of* him. I certainly don't know the man himself."

Faye looked around then leaned forward. "I understand he was married."

Delia had wondered about that. She assumed he was in his early thirties. A man of his age and station should have married long ago. She waited to hear Mena's response.

"Barbara died several years ago. It must have been five, no six years now." Mena's eyes dropped to the burgundy and white chair. She looked both directions down the hall before leaning toward Delia. "Bennie told me the chair you sit in now belonged to her."

Delia felt herself stiffen. She could hear the brusque sound of the captain's voice when he came upon her sitting in the chair. No wonder he seemed angry.

"It was in Glennon House when he arrived. He ordered it be removed immediately." Mena was practically whispering.

Delia wondered if he was aware the chair had been moved to Glennon Hall before he saw her sitting in it. Given his reaction, she doubted it now.

Faye whispered something back but Delia couldn't hear her over the voices in the hallway as their colleagues arrived. It was time for the meeting. As she stood to follow the others to the meeting room, she debated once again if she should approach the new principal. Perhaps he was more understanding than she originally thought?

CHAPTER EIGHTEEN

Delia had no idea what the principal's schedule was like. She approached the Biltmore Building with trepidation in between her classes. Part of her hoped the man wasn't in his office. Once inside the old building named for a past trustee of the school, she paused in the entrance to get her bearings. There were signs pointing to the registrar's office and the textbook library. It wasn't until she moved partway down the hall that she saw the signs directing her to the principal's office on the second floor.

She ascended the stairs slowly, still debating her decision to speak with the principal. The door to the outer office was open when she reached it. Delia squared her shoulders and stepped inside. The look of surprise on Bennie's face told her that he didn't often see faculty in his doorway.

"Miss Markham." Bennie stood so quickly he nearly knocked over his chair. "Is something the matter?"

Delia glanced to her right. The door to the principal's office was closed. "I was wondering if Principal Glennon might have a moment to speak with me."

It took Bennie a moment to answer her. His eyes shifted from Delia to the principal's door and back again.

He swallowed with effort. "Yes, miss. Let me just check on that. If you'll excuse me for a moment."

Delia remained where she was. Bennie stopped at the principal's door and turned back to Delia. She knew his attempt at a smile was meant to comfort but the effort failed. He tapped quietly and entered at the sound of a muffled word. He opened the door only enough to slip through. The door closed behind him with a soft click.

She didn't understand whatever Bennie said. The voice that came after was louder. When Bennie slipped back through the door, Delia was studying the ceiling with interest as though she hadn't heard the principal's short-tempered comment.

"Principal Glennon can see you now, miss." Bennie remained near the open door.

Delia crossed over and entered the office. She heard the soft sound of the door closing behind her as she studied the room. One of the walls was lined completely with a bookcase. The others held paintings of men she presumed were his relatives. Past principals of the school who once sat in the very same office. The current principal was behind a massive desk. He was watching her with interest.

Delia moved to stand in front of his desk. "Thank you for seeing me, Principal Glennon."

"Acting principal." He rested his arms on the desk in front of him. "To what do I owe this pleasure, Miss Markham?"

"I hoped to speak with you about the incident last evening."

"Indeed? And which incident might that be?" The narrowing of his eyes belied the slight curve of his lips.

"With Willie and Harry, the students that were caught stealing food."

"Indeed. And your interest in the incident. Are you concerned about the losses of food?"

Delia felt her chin go up. "My concern, sir, is for the students."

"How so?" He shifted back in his chair as though awaiting her answer.

Delia chose her words carefully. "As you may know, my cousin is the head chef here. Both Willie and Harry worked as servers in the dining hall to help pay for their schooling. An admirable undertaking, would you not agree?"

"Admirable." The tone of his voice made it clear the activity did not rank highly with him.

"They were also my typewriting students. I can attest to their studious nature in class," Delia said.

The last wasn't completely honest. The two boys were more apt to debate the outcomes of recent baseball games than they were to apply themselves to their assignments.

He steepled his hands together. "And your intentions with this visit, Miss Markham. What is your hope for the outcome?"

"I understand that you haven't turned the boys over the police?" When he didn't respond, she continued. "I hoped to sway you toward leniency in their reprimand."

His brows went up. "Reprimand? They're thieves. They deserve far more than a reprimand."

"My understanding is that they stole to support their families," Delia countered. "Surely that should hold some weight in your decision."

The look on his face told her it did not. "They need to be punished for their actions. While others are crossing the ocean and taking up arms, these two remain here and take food from others. If I had my way, they'd be joining their brothers in the war. All of the other men who are fighting for our country. Let them see firsthand the sacrifices that are being made."

It was the manner in which he said it that gave her pause. "If you had your way?"

His eyes flicked away from hers for a moment before returning. "My sister does not want the misdeeds of those two tied to the name of this school."

Of course. She should have considered as much. "You plan to offer them leniency?"

"I didn't say that. If possible, I'll have those two in uniform."

"Surely not if it causes their families to suffer?"

"You overstep your duties, Miss Markham. The discipline of students falls under the principal. I believe that ends this conversation."

"But, sir. Although egregious, their misdeeds were limited to the pilfering of food in the middle of the night. Technically, they were caught moving food from one building on campus to another."

His eyes locked onto hers. "You sound as though you have some special knowledge of their actions."

Delia held his gaze. "Perhaps I have difficulty sleeping at night from my memories in the service and I find a late-night stroll soothing, Captain."

She knew her arrow hit the mark when she saw the flicker of anger in his eyes.

He pushed himself up from his chair and stood glaring at her. "Once again, you overstep your bounds, Yeoman!"

"Captain!" Bennie stood in the open doorway.

Delia and the captain remained where they were, their focus on each other.

"What is it?" Wes ground out.

Bennie stepped into the room. "The groundskeeper. Arch Keaton, sir. He's just been arrested for murder."

CHAPTER NINETEEN

Though the preparations for the noonday meal were underway, only the sounds of the women working could be heard in the kitchen. No one was speaking as Delia burst into the room looking for Hazel. All heads turned toward her but one. Hazel stood in the middle of the room staring at a wall. She had her apron pulled up and was wiping her hands with it.

Delia moved to her cousin and reached for Hazel's elbow.

"Come with me," she said gently.

Hazel didn't argue. She blindly followed Delia to the storeroom. Delia opened the door and nudged Hazel inside before closing the door behind them.

"Tell me what happened."

Hazel shook her head. "It can't be. They have to know he wouldn't do it."

"Hazel!" It was said sharply on purpose. Hazel's eyes snapped to hers. "I cannot help if you won't talk to me. Do you understand?"

Hazel pressed her lips together and nodded. Her hands reached for her apron again.

"Tell me what you know," Delia asked again. "Who was killed?"

"His name is Frank. Was Frank. Frank Lawton." Hazel's eyes were wide with fear as she pulled her apron up and knotted the fabric in her hands.

"Was he from Glennon?"

Hazel nodded mutely.

"How did he die?"

"Poison." Hazel looked past Delia's shoulder as though seeing something there. "They said it was arsenate of lead."

Delia tried to remember everything she'd ever heard of the common insecticide. "Arch used it at the school?"

"He said it was cheaper than Paris green. He buys the powdered form because he uses so much of it. Just everywhere, really. In the garden for the potato and cabbage worms. Then there are the armyworms. He uses it on the fruit trees." Hazel's eyes returned to Delia. They no longer looked empty and lost. Now they were pleading. "You'll help him, won't you?"

Delia knew it wasn't the time to argue that success with two young food thieves would hardly qualify her to find a murderer. "Why would anyone think Arch might kill the man?"

A deep furrow appeared on Hazel's forehead. The apron slipped from her hands as she wrapped her arms around herself. "Frank's wife."

"Excuse me?"

"It was when he was a young man. Arch used to court Sadie Lawton. Before she was married, of course. She chose Frank over Arch." Hazel shook her head slowly. "She married above her station. Frank owned the Electric Shoe Repair in town. He made really good money from it. That's what attracted Sadie to it. Everyone in town knew it, of course. With the money from his business, she probably never had to work another day of her life. Probably has servants to do everything."

Delia tried to piece together what Hazel was saying. It didn't make sense. "If what you say is true, this was many years ago. Why would anyone think Arch would kill him now?"

The fear returned to Hazel's eyes.

"Hazel, you have to tell me. What is it?"

Hazel's hands came up to her mouth. "Arch got into an argument with Frank in town."

"This was recently?"

Hazel nodded. Her eyes looked huge above the small hands covering her mouth.

Delia thought back to her late-night excursions. She encountered Arch more than once. Was it Wednesday when she found him near his outbuilding where he keeps the insecticide? She knew for sure it was him. He'd confessed as much to her.

Hazel's voice interrupted her thoughts. "He didn't do. Arch wouldn't."

Delia let that go for now. "Why does the name Lawton sound familiar to me?"

Hazel's hands reached for her apron again. "Probably because of Carl. Frank's son. Carl was a student at Glennon Normal School."

***

The hardest part of her next class was not checking the time. Delia knew the students would notice if her eyes continued to find their way to the clock on the wall behind them. She spent a few minutes after the class erasing the chalk from the board to give her students time to file out of the room. As soon as she was certain they were gone, she went down the grand staircase and made her way across campus to the library.

Mena was at the front desk speaking with a student when Delia found her. After one look at Delia, she excused herself from the student and came around the desk.

Mena's eyes scanned the room. "Over here."

Delia followed her from the main library room to a hallway that led to a recreation hall. When Mena took a seat at the end of the hallway, Delia sat next to her.

"You look as though you ran all the way over here." Mena's eyes went up to Delia's hair.

"I believe I did." Delia's hands rose automatically and began tucking loose hairs back into their pins. "Have you heard?"

"About Arch?" Mena's eyes held understanding. "I imagine Hazel must be beside herself."

Delia had wondered if anyone knew of their relationship.

Mena checked the hall to make sure they were alone. "Her secret is safe with me. I've never told anyone."

"But you knew?"

"Not with any certainty. I suspected. I saw them look at each other once. It was so sweet." Mena sounded wistful.

"Can you tell me anything about the man that died?" Delia tucked another strand of hair into a pin.

"Frank Lawton? You know that his son used to be a student here?"

Delia made a noise indicating yes.

"Frank and Sadie Lawton own the Electric Shoe Repair. They do a very nice business there." A small furrow appeared briefly between Mena's brows. "Years ago, he used to have a partner in the shop."

Delia felt her head for more loose hairs. Finding none, she dropped her hands to her lap. "What happened to him?"

"That's just it. I've never heard any gossip. Not about that, at any rate." Mena's eyes darted around the hall. "His name was Bob Hinkle. Once he and Frank parted ways, Bob took a job here."

Delia wasn't expecting to hear that. "Here at the normal school? Doing what?"

"Night watchman. I imagine it was a difficult transition for him but at the time I suspect he needed the money."

"Why did he leave here?"

"That I don't know." Mena made a face of apology.

"It's alright." Delia thought of Bennie. "I may know someone who does."

Mena leaned forward and whispered. "There was a mention in the newspaper once about Bob. The police had to be called to his house."

"For what?"

Mena pressed her lips together as she leaned back in her chair. "The newspaper said his wife chose not to file any charges."

Delia understood what that meant. "I have to get back to Glennon Hall. I have another class starting soon."

Mena stood when Delia did. "I feel so badly about Arch. If there is anything I can do to help, please let me know."

Delia thanked Mena and quickly made the return trip to her classroom. Just as she neared the entrance to Glennon Hall, she saw Bennie exiting. She remained where she was until he reached her.

"Miss Markham. I wish to apologize." Bennie glanced around them. "On behalf of Captain Glennon."

Delia smiled at a group of students then moved over to the side out of hearing range. "There's no need for that, I assure you." When he tried to disagree, she interrupted him. "Bennie, I need your help."

She saw that she had his attention. "I know that you have access to the employee records." She waited for him to nod his agreement. "I need you to find one in particular for me."

Delia gave him the name then excused herself for class. She had just enough time to tidy her hair again before the students began filing in. She spent the entire period hoping her distraction wasn't as obvious to her students as it was to her. She followed the last student from the room at the end of the class. As she descended the stairs, she debated going to the principal's office to find Bennie.

She was happy to find him just inside the entrance of Glennon Hall. "You found something?"

He nodded toward the fireplace. They crossed over and took a seat. Since Bennie sat on the sofa, Delia took the burgundy and white chair across from him.

"I cannot stay long," Bennie said. "I looked up the record for Bob Hinkle. He was, indeed, the night watchman here for a short time."

"Why did he leave?"

"No definitive reason was given."

It was the way he said it. She could tell he was holding back information. "But?"

"His record indicates that Mr. Hinkle often had health issues." Bennie made a face. "It said he was indisposed."

"Indisposed," Delia repeated.

Bennie made another face. "What do you suppose that means?"

Delia didn't have a chance to answer.

"What the devil are you up to now?" Wes demanded.

Delia flashed her eyes at Bennie then shifted them to the entrance before standing to face the irate principal. From the periphery of her view, she saw Bennie steal away from the building.

"Captain Glennon. I do not appreciate your tone." The surprise she saw in his eyes emboldened her to continue. "I do not believe that Arch Keaton is a murderer." She sincerely hoped he wasn't.

Only part of his bluster returned. "What are you planning to do about it?" His eyes narrowed. "You aren't planning any more late-night walks, are you?"

"If needs must, Captain."

He opened his mouth to speak then noticed a group of students gathering to watch. He lifted his brows and offered a stern look. The students began to scatter.

He lowered his voice. "Darkness can hide all manner of bad things, Miss Markham. Things that could harm you. I would not wish to have that on my conscience."

"I absolve you of any responsibility, Captain."

His hand came up to rub his face in exasperation. "That is not the point."

"I promised my help, Captain. I will not go back on my word." Delia began walking away.

His words stopped her. "Even if the man in question specifically said he doesn't want you in danger either?"

She spun around to face him. "You've spoken with Arch?"

"I went to see him at the jail." He put his hand up to stop her next question. "He is fine. As fine as a man can be when charged with murder."

"What did he say? Did he give any indication if the poison that was used might have come from here?"

"My concerns exactly, Miss Markham. According to Arch, it was possible small amounts of poison could have been taken from his stock over time but there was never a large amount. There was never a noticeable amount taken from the school's supply."

CHAPTER TWENTY

As soon as her final class for the day was over, Delia prepared to leave the normal school. Although she was finally learning her way around the campus rather well, she had yet to spend the necessary time exploring the town of Glennon to navigate its streets as easily. At most, she knew her way to the church that she and Hazel attended the previous Sunday.

As she reached the edge of the campus in the front of Glennon Hall, she paused to get her bearings. From where she stood, there were roads leading away from the school in multiple directions. Those roads were lined with houses located on the northern point of the town of Glennon. She knew that the main road leading from the campus to downtown Glennon was well kept and modern. Many others that led away from that road into the lesser occupied areas most often were not.

She waited until the trolley arrived on schedule in front of the school. According to Bennie, the route between the town and the school still ran regularly, even with the conservation efforts. There were too many employees and students that relied upon it and too many businesses in town that relied on the patronage of those from the school.

Following Bennie's instructions, she managed to make her

way to the tree-lined road where Elbert Greenlee lived. The trolley didn't take her to his modest home. It dropped her off at the end of his unpaved road. She walked the short distance from the corner to his house grateful that they hadn't received much rain lately. Removing a layer of dust from her boots should prove easier than removing mud.

The Greenlees lived in a two-story house that had been painted white. The posts supporting the front porch were painted white with a dark green trim to give it a decorative touch. She climbed the wood steps leading to the porch and tapped on the outer screen door. There was no answer.

Delia stepped away from the door and looked both directions down the road. There was no one about to ask if the night watchman was home. She decided to try again. This time she opened the screen door first and knocked loudly on the wood door.

The man that answered looked rumpled from sleep. Elbert Greenlee ran a hand through his hair as he peered at Delia curiously.

"Mr. Greenlee?"

"Yes, ma'am. My wife isn't home if you're interested in selling something." Elbert reached for the door to close it as he began to turn away.

"No, Mr. Greenlee." It came out louder than she intended but had the effect she needed. The man froze in place with his arm in the air.

"I'm here about Arch Keaton." Delia watched curiosity chase away confusion on the man's face. "My name is Miss Delia Markham. I'm Hazel's cousin."

Understanding replaced any remaining fragments of confusion. Delia wondered how much of a secret Arch and Hazel really were.

"I'm very sorry about his situation, but I'm not certain how I can help." He offered a shrug of apology.

Delia considered her options. Asking to speak with the man alone in his house was summarily rejected. It wasn't the reputation she wanted to earn.

"If you wouldn't mind." She motioned to the porch. "I won't take long."

When Elbert stepped outside, she continued. "I apologize for coming unannounced. I assumed that you would sleep during the day but would be awake in the afternoon before your shift tonight."

"Yes, miss. I woke not long ago. My wife went into town to pick up a few things at the store there." Elbert looked toward the road as though hoping his wife would appear and save him from the woman on the porch.

"I understand that a man named Bob Hinkle used to work for you as a night watchman at the school. Can you tell me about that?"

She watched the confusion return to his face. "Why was he asked to leave?"

"Oh, that." Elbert rubbed a hand against the stubble on his face. "Well, he was often indisposed."

"Are you saying that he was drunk?" Delia offered a small smile at the look of surprise on his face. "This conversation would go more quickly if we could speak a common language."

"Yes, miss. He was either drunk or sleeping it off. I felt sorry for him at first, of course."

"Because of the business he used to be in?" Delia guessed.

Elbert looked impressed. "Exactly. He was a big man then. Made good money with the shoe repair. I thought it would be a good fit for him at the school being as how he lives so close to it. That is, he did after he lost all his money. Had to move into a different neighborhood, as you might imagine."

"What happened with his business? Do you know?"

Elbert made face. "Be hard not to. It's all Bob talked about when he was drinking. Of course, I only know what he told me."

"His side of the story," Delia murmured.

"Right. He'd get into his rye whiskey and go on about it for hours. About how Frank Lawton cheated him out of business."

"He didn't go into specifics?"

"Claimed it was how the business document was written up. I'm guessing Bob didn't read it closely enough when he first signed it. Frank was giving Bob money from the business. Bob just assumed it was from what they made there."

"From the business proceeds," Delia supplied.

Elbert pointed at her. "Right, that's it. Bob thought it was just the business proceeds from the earnings."

"It wasn't?"

"No, miss. It was Frank's way of getting Bob out of the business. Not only that, but Frank did it at a fraction of the cost."

"He cheated the man out of business?" Delia remembered what Elbert said about the contract. "No. He had the contract written up to buy Bob out of business."

"Smart of him, wasn't it? Frank used Bob's money to start the business but then paid him off at one tenth of what Bob put in. Frank owned the whole lot of it after that."

"Bob didn't take him to court?"

"Claims he tried, but he lost. The contract was written up that way. Bob signed it."

In the distance Delia could hear the whistle of the trolley.

Elbert heard it also. "That's your ride, miss. You'll want to catch it or you'll need to wait for the next trip around to make it back to the school."

Delia didn't want to miss her ride but not because she wanted to get back to the campus. "Do you know where Bob Hinkle is working now?"

"I've seen him delivering coal. He works for Speers. Not that it's likely you'll find him engaged in such an industrious undertaking much of the time." The corners of Elbert's mouth turned down. "From what I've heard, the man rarely shows up for work. And if he did, there's no way you can be chasing him down while he's doing it."

Delia knew he was right. "Today is Friday. Even if he only worked a few hours this week, he'll be wanting any pay that's owed to him."

It took him a moment to catch on. When he did, he shook his head. "And no doubt it won't be long in his pocket before he hands it over to the barkeeper. Even if you waylay him at the main office when he shows up for his pay, I still don't think it's a good idea. The man is a hothead under any condition whether he is drinking or not. It's just not safe, miss."

Delia asked for the directions to the main office. Elbert Greenlee was still shaking his head as she moved quickly to catch the trolley. He told her that Bob would need to fill his supply truck at Speers Run outside of town to make deliveries, but Mr. Speers kept his office in town. It was where he conducted his business transactions. Delia alighted from the trolley several minutes later just a half a block away.

Rather than walking to Speers, she turned to look in the window of the grocer. It occurred to her that she should pick up some tea. Hazel's tea tin was nearly empty. The sign on the wall behind the counter showed the prices for some of the goods. Delia winced at the number for loose tea. Forty-five cents per pound. It seemed that prices during the war only ever went up. She wondered if the end of war might mean a return to the former rates.

The sound of a truck passing by interrupted her thoughts. She turned to watch it. She didn't have to guess that it might stop at the main office for Speers Coal Company. The form of the Quad truck indicated its primary function was to transport heavy loads. That ability is what made the vehicle and others like it so popular for the war effort.

Delia began walking toward the office. She was close enough to see the man who climbed from the truck enter the coal company. He didn't match the description she was given. She slowed her steps and stopped in front of another shop.

This one had a display of hats in the window. Most were women's hats but there were also several hats for men including one similar to what Arch wore.

She turned back to check the activity in front of the coal company office. A man was walking toward her from the other direction. Delia moved quickly to intercept him before he reached the front door.

"Mr. Hinkle. If I might have a word?" Delia positioned herself between Bob Hinkle and the doorway to his weekly pay.

A scowl contorted a heavily lined face with unkempt facial hair. "What's this?"

"I understand your former business partner was murdered." Delia watched the man's bloodshot eyes shift to the door behind her.

"What's it to you?"

"Answer my questions and your pay will be in your hands within moments," Delia said. "It stands to reason that you knew Frank Lawton better than many. Aside from yourself, who else would wish to see him dead?"

A momentary flash of confusion crossed Bob Hinkle's face as he tried to follow Delia's meaning. When her words penetrated his fogged brain, his scowl deepened as a flush mottled his cheeks. "See here, now. Who are you to make such a claim? I am a respected man of this community."

Although he attempted to move around her, Delia stepped back to block his entrance. "I understand you often have time on your hands, Mr. Hinkle."

"I can hardly be blamed for the coal shortage," he spat out. "I'm entitled to the meager earnings of a reduced schedule because of it. Let me pass."

This time he managed to brush past her though Delia didn't put up a fight. She assumed she heard as much as he planned to tell. She retraced her footsteps quickly not wishing to miss the trolley. She wanted to speak with Hazel at home before she had to go out again and she still needed to do a little shopping first.

CHAPTER TWENTY-ONE

Delia knew Hazel was home the moment she opened the rear door of the house. It was the smell that greeted her as she stepped into the kitchen.

"You're home then." Hazel stood next to the gas cabinet range.

Delia slid out of her walking coat and crossed the kitchen on her way to her room. "Not for long. I bought some tea. I'll put it away in a moment."

When Delia returned to the kitchen, Hazel already had the loose tea in the tin and was pulling dishes from the cabinet.

"I can help." Delia stopped in the middle of the kitchen. Hazel was moving about so quickly, she didn't want to get in her way. "Perhaps you should sit for a few moments. You have been on your feet all day."

Hazel shook her head as she moved back to the range. "I don't want my thoughts to be idle."

"You're worried about Arch."

Hazel froze for just a moment before turning back to Delia. "Have you learned anything?"

"I would not wish to raise your hopes needlessly," Delia warned.

"Tell me." Hazel lifted her apron and began to wipe her hands.

Delia walked over to the range. After checking the pot of simmering stew, she moved the tea kettle to a burner. She used the flame from the burner under the stew to light a match for the water.

"I have managed to learn a little about the victim. Have you ever been to his shoe repair shop?" Delia went to the cabinet.

"It's been years. That was before Arch and I. Well." Hazel's fingers began to worry the edge of her apron.

"Before you were together," Delia finished for her. She took two teacups out and set them down before reaching for the tea tin. "You knew he had a partner?"

"Yes, of course. What about it?" Hazel joined Delia and nudged her out of the way as she reached for the tea tin. She took out the measuring spoon.

Although Delia was not large for a woman, Hazel's slight frame still had little effect. Delia held her ground and reached for the tea ball to hold it for Hazel. "I'm told the victim cheated the former partner out of the business."

Hazel's hand shook spreading loose tea everywhere. "That must be it. You have to tell the police."

Delia gave an apologetic look. "That is why I did not want to raise your hopes. The police would already know about the former partner."

"Oh. Yes, of course." Hazel began brushing the tea into a pile on the porcelain workspace of the cabinet. A tall piece of furniture made of waxed oak with a white enamel interior, it held many of the kitchen necessities.

"It still gives me a starting point," Delia said. "In fact, I spoke with Mr. Hinkle not long ago."

"You did?" Hazel abandoned her efforts with the tea and put one hand on Delia's arm. "You will be safe, won't you?"

"Of course."

"But Delia, whoever killed Frank Lawton will not wish to be found out. He might hurt you also."

"I am aware of that."

"I don't want you in harm's way."

"I can take care of myself." Delia measured the tea into the tea ball.

"You were nearly killed just this summer."

"But I was not killed. As I said, I can take care of myself." Delia put the ball into the teapot and carried it over to the range. "Besides, the murderer may well be a woman."

"What? A woman?" Hazel followed her. "Surely not."

"Frank Lawton was poisoned," Delia pointed out.

"You think that's important?" Hazel lifted her spoon and stirred the stew.

Delia reached for the kettle when it whistled. "That is what I wish to find out. Poison seems more of a weapon for a woman. We shall see. In the meantime, I need to learn more about Bob Hinkle. I understand that he lives very near the campus."

"That he does. Promise me you won't be hurt." Hazel set the spoon down and turned to Delia. "I want Arch to be free, but I don't want you injured in the process."

"I promise I will take care." Delia returned to the cabinet for the teacups. "Tell me about the coal shortage here."

"Coal shortage?" Hazel remained near the range but watched Delia. "It was troublesome last winter. We all made do, of course. Just as we should. The boys fighting the war needed it more than we did."

"But this year? I understood that areas such as Glennon shouldn't have as much trouble."

Hazel lifted the teapot and carried it to the table. "That is my understanding as well. The larger cities may suffer but areas such as ours with our own local supplies shouldn't be as hard hit. We all have been so careful to follow the recommendations to economize since last year."

"That's what I thought." Delia set the teacups on the table. "And yet, our Mr. Hinkle was emphatic that his supply runs were suffering from the shortage. He made it sound as though that was the reason he wasn't working as much."

"I know that look." Hazel pointed at her cousin. "You plan to go out again tonight."

Delia smiled. "It would be a shame not to wear my new cap."

***

Delia dressed with care before leaving Hazel's house after dinner. The short walk to the school campus didn't take long. When she reached the main walkway, she turned toward the auditorium. Others were also moving in the same direction for the same reason.

"Delia, you made it." Mena excused herself from a group of people.

"I would not wish to miss a performance hosted by our committee," Delia said. "As you know, it is mandatory that we participate."

"We should probably get to our seats." Mena greeted a group of students with a smile and a nod.

"I have heard promising things about the performance this evening. I have a fondness for contralto voices." Delia fell into step with Mena. She nodded to several people as they passed them. "Where should we sit?"

"I was thinking the far corner might be the best location." Mena pointed before turning in that direction. "It will allow you a better viewing advantage."

Delia followed Mena into the auditorium. There was an area at the opposite end for the performers. Delia could barely see it over the crowds of people. Much of the auditorium was filled with chairs for the audience. Many of the attendees were already seated. Others were intent on taking their seats. The entire auditorium buzzed with the sound of voices.

Delia stopped next to the chairs that Mena indicated then noted the close proximity to the exit. "A most excellent idea."

"I understand the singer has performed with several well-known orchestras," Mena said as she surveyed the people in the room. "She is to be accompanied by both a pianist and a cellist."

"Sounds like we're in for an enjoyable evening." Delia took her seat on the end of the row.

Mena was seated next to her one chair in from the end. "The performance should begin soon. There will be an intermission about halfway through. The program should conclude sometime after eleven."

Delia smiled as she watched the latecomers take their seats. "Thank you for this."

The lights in the auditorium dimmed. Delia sat through several minutes of the performance until she was sure it was dusk. Just before the singer ended another song, she slid from her seat.

"Be safe," Mena said quietly.

Delia was gone a moment later. She moved quickly out of the main auditorium area and went down a long hall. When she reached the end, she opened a door to a closet and stepped inside. The package on a shelf with rolls of crepe toilet paper told her that Hazel had been there as planned. Although crammed with supplies, the space inside the closet was large enough for Delia to change into her sailor's uniform. She covered her hair with the new cap and used the rear employee exit to leave the building.

Avoiding the main walkways, she made it across the campus and to the main street in front of Glennon Hall. Following Hazel's directions, she turned left and walked for several blocks. Whenever possible, she used the light from the street lamps. Once she reached the road she was looking for and turned, she used her flashlight.

The house where Bob Hinkle lived was small. She guessed it had four rooms total. Delia stopped a distance away and shut off her light as she waited. From what she could tell when using her flashlight, the Hinkle house did not have close neighbors.

Now that she was here, she debated her initial reason for coming. She hoped to speak with Bob Hinkle once he'd spent his meager pay at the local saloon. According to Elbert Greenlee, the watchman supervisor, Bob was very talkative when he had too much to drink. She wanted to use that to her advantage to question the man. However, a light from one of the rooms told her that Mrs. Hinkle was probably awake. She considered trying to speak with her first before Mr. Hinkle returned.

A nearby sound told her that she'd missed her chance. The voice she heard was full of anger. A figure burst from the darkness shouting to himself the entire time. Though his gait was unsteady, he moved with great speed toward the home she was watching. Before Delia could intercept Bob Hinkle, he had thrown the front door open and lurched inside. The door slammed behind him with force.

Delia left her place in the shadows and approached the Hinkle house. She could hear shouting from inside. There were two voices, a man and a woman. Something hard crashed against a wall. A moment later, there was the sound of glass breaking.

"Miss Delia."

Delia whirled around toward the voice behind her and switched on her flashlight. "Sam? Is that you?"

"Yes, miss. I saw you leave the school. I thought you might need help."

She could hear the fear in Sam's voice as he turned toward the Hinkle home.

"Sam, listen to me. Do you think you can hurry back to the school and collect the night watchman? Tell him we need the police here. Tell him to call the police on the telephone. Do you understand?"

"Yes, miss."

With that he was gone. Delia remained where she was and listened to the shouting inside. It seemed as though she waited for hours for the police wagon to appear though she knew it was a matter of minutes. Delia returned to the darkness out of the range of the street light as soon as she heard the wagon approach. The policemen wasted no time reaching the front door. Within moments they were inside.

Delia found her way back toward the school in the darkness, grateful when she reached the street lamps of the main road. Her fingers fumbled through her change of clothes in the supply closet. She used the water from the slop-hopper to wet her hands before smoothing her hair. After tucking several stray strands back into their pins, she emerged into the hallway of the auditorium and returned to her seat. She applauded with everyone else as the lights came back on.

CHAPTER TWENTY-TWO

Early Saturday morning, Delia made a return trip to the Hinkle home. This time, she walked right up to the front door and knocked. The woman that answered it looked at her suspiciously. Delia forced herself not to wince at the discoloration around the woman's eye. Ella Hinkle's gaze swept Delia from her head to her toes and back again. Suspicion turned to dismissal.

"I can't afford to make any donations." Ella began to close the door.

Delia took a step forward. "Mrs. Hinkle, I know how you acquired the bruises."

The suspicious glare returned. "Who are you?"

"If you let me in, I'll explain that. And tell you why I was here last evening."

Ella pointed a finger at Delia. "It was you who called the police."

"It seemed like a good idea at the time."

Ella stared at her a moment before turning from the door.

Delia chose to take the open door as an invitation. She closed the door behind her and followed Ella into the kitchen.

"I can't offer you anything." Ella stood in the middle of the room.

Delia was reminded that the woman once had a much different life when her husband owned a business. "A chair would do nicely."

Delia sat on one of the chairs next to a small, round kitchen table. Ella took the other chair a moment later.

"I wanted to speak with your husband last night. I was outside waiting for him but he appeared from a direction I wasn't expecting. I'm sorry that I couldn't get to him in time to stop him," Delia said.

"It wouldn't have mattered. As drunk as he was, he might have mistaken you for me." Ella pointed at her swollen eye. "Then you would have one too."

Delia looked at the potato bin near the wall behind Ella. She stood and crossed over to it. After taking a potato out she went to the white enamel kitchen cabinet to find a knife.

"Has he always been like this? Or was it just since he lost his half of the business to Frank Lawton?" Delia pared the potato then searched the cabinet for a grater.

"Not before I married him. He never hurt me before we married. Of course, I knew even before then that he was a weak man. At the time, I thought it meant I would be safe from such treatment. That was my mistake. I discovered that he's only brave when he's dealing with an even weaker woman. One who has no other options."

Delia finished grating the potato and brought it over to the table. "You don't believe your husband killed Frank Lawton?"

"Thanks." A faint smile touched Ella's lips as she reached for the grated potato. "Bob never did anything to Frank. Never said a word to the man when Frank cheated him out of the business. Never took him to court. He knew he was a fool for signing the contract. He knew he'd lose the court case."

"Why did Frank take the business from him?" Delia helped Ella apply the potato around her eye.

"He was a drunkard, even then. That's why Frank wanted him out. I couldn't blame Frank for that. I wanted out too." Ella's fingers pressed gently against the potato near her eye. "I don't think Bob could have killed Frank. To be honest, it would have required too much thought."

"Are the police going to keep him this time?" Delia asked.

Ella's head shook but only slightly, as though the movement caused her pain. "They won't keep him long. They never do."

***

Delia took the trolley to town. The Electric Shoe Repair was located on a side street right off of Main. Delia climbed the cement steps and entered the shop. Bells on the door jingled as she opened and closed it. There was a woman in the corner.

"Just a moment," she said over the sound of the electric sewing machine.

Delia read the signs on the walls while she waited. There were prices for repairing soles and heels. One sign suggested using rubber soles instead of leather to save money. Another sign promised to turn old shoes into new and that the work would be completed while the customer waited.

The sound of the sewing machine stopped. "Can I help you?"

Delia offered a friendly smile. "I was hoping to speak with Mrs. Lawton. Is she in?"

"You found her." Mrs. Lawton's eyes dropped to Delia's shoes. She held the pair of shoes in her hands that she just completed repairing.

"Oh, I'm not here for a repair." The image of a rich woman with many servants painted by Hazel danced through her mind. She dismissed it. "I was hoping to speak with you about your son, Carl."

"He isn't here." Sadie Lawton carried the pair of shoes over to a counter and set them down. She immediately lifted a pair of women's boots and returned to the sewing machine.

"Do you know when he might return?" Delia closed the distance between them as the woman settled back in her seat behind the machine.

"No. What's it to you?" The sewing machine buzzed into life.

Delia raised her voice. "I am the typewriting teacher at the normal school. I understand Carl was expected to return this term."

"He's been busy," Sadie shouted over the sound of the machine.

Delia remained where she was until the woman finished with the first boot. When the noise from the machine stopped, she spoke again. "Very impressive machine."

"It is." Sadie pushed herself up from the chair and carried one of the boots over to a workbench. She used a small tool to repair one of the button hooks then carried the boot to the counter.

"Your shop seems very busy, Mrs. Lawton. How many other employees do you have working here?" Delia asked.

"Just me." Sadie returned to the sewing machine. A moment later, it buzzed into life again.

"Does Carl help you?" Delia persisted.

"He used to. He's too busy now."

"I imagine losing his father would be difficult," Delia said loudly. "No doubt, he has been dealing with the arrangements."

The sewing machine continued to run but Sadie didn't respond.

"Can you tell me when Carl will return? I would like to speak with him about his classes," Delia said.

"He hasn't been here today," Sadie said.

"Do you expect him?" Delia asked.

Sadie's head shook but her hands never stopped their work. "No. He said he would be too busy."

"Perhaps tomorrow? Will he be attending church with you?"

"I won't be able to make it to church. I have too much work to do here." The sewing machine stopped. Sadie stood and crossed over to the counter to set the second boot down next to the first.

Delia watched her reach for another pair of shoes. "Please tell him that I wish to speak with him when he does return."

Sadie didn't speak as she returned to the sewing machine. A moment later, it buzzed into life.

Delia left the repair shop to catch the trolley. She needed to get back to Hazel's. After a quick change, she walked to Glennon Hall. It was full of activity as students moved through the hallways on their way to the various parlors where faculty waited to greet them.

Delia joined the commercial department faculty in one of the rooms. Faye greeted her as soon as she entered the room.

"There you are. I was beginning to worry. It wouldn't do to miss the faculty reception for the students." Faye motioned to a table behind them that held trays of food. "Your cousin outdid herself this time."

Delia didn't have to wonder why. Hazel's love of cooking was deeply ingrained. It offered not only the challenges she loved but the solace she needed during difficult times.

"Faye, do you have a moment?" Earl Gordon stopped next to them.

Delia smiled a greeting at the head of the commercial department and excused herself. From the corner of her eye, she saw a movement near the door. It was young Sam. He waved her over.

"Sam, you surprised me showing up like that last night. You shouldn't be out so late."

"It's alright, miss. I know my way about even in the dark." Sam led Delia from the room to an alcove in the hallway. "The police were here."

"Police? When?"

"Earlier, miss. In the morning. They were looking all around." Sam had his cap in his hands.

"Looking at what, exactly?"

"Arch's buildings. You know, where he keeps his supplies."

"The poison." It made sense. The police were strengthening their case against the groundskeeper.

"Yes, miss." Sam twisted his cap. "It isn't fair. He didn't do it. He wouldn't. I know the poison wasn't taken from us. Arch said so when the police took him away."

"I know, Sam." Even as she said it, Delia wondered when she'd started believing it. When she knew that Arch was innocent. She put her hand on Sam's shoulder. "Did the police speak with you?"

Sam nodded. "On account of me working with him so much. They wanted to know if I heard the argument Arch had with the man who died."

Delia watched the boy's lips tremble for just a moment before he pressed them together.

"You heard it?"

"Yes, miss. We went into town to pick up supplies, Arch and me. That's where we saw him."

"What did the men argue about?"

The cap was now in a knot. "It was nothing, miss."

"Sam, I can't help if I don't know what's going on." She deliberately made her voice sound stern. It did the job.

"It was the other man's fault. He laughed at Arch saying as how he'd have to go to war. Arch ignored him, of course. He's no coward." Sam's voice grew louder with his impassioned show of loyalty for his friend.

"Shh. Of course he isn't." Delia looked around. Everyone was so excited about their evening, no one was paying attention to them. "Then why did they argue?"

Sam's eyes dropped to the knotted cap in his hands. "I can't really say, miss."

"But Sam..."

His eyes came up. "No, miss. Arch said I wasn't ever to use such words in front of ladies."

Delia inwardly debated forcing Sam to break his code of conduct when a thought came to her. "Was it about Miss Hazel?"

Sam's eyes widened.

Suddenly it made sense. "Mr. Lawton said something impolite about Hazel and Arch?"

The red hue that infused Sam's face confirmed her suspicion. Delia put her hand on Sam's shoulder.

"It's alright, Sam. I'll tell Arch that you refused to tell me."

Sam dropped his eyes to the twisted cap in his hands. "I'm sorry that I dropped your plate in the dining hall."

"I already forgave you for that, remember?"

"Yes, miss. It's just that they were talking about going away to the service."

Delia remembered. At the time, she was glad of Sam's distraction. It took the focus of the discussion away from her activities in the service. It didn't take her long to connect the two conversations. "You're worried about Arch leaving?"

"I was worried about him being drafted," Sam mumbled.

And now he was worried about the man being convicted. "Let's focus on his current troubles first, shall we?"

Sam lifted his eyes to hers. She saw hope in them as he realized that they both sought the same goal. She smiled as she gently squeezed his shoulder. "Off with you then. I have to get back to my meeting."

Delia spent the afternoon making small talk with her colleagues and students. As much as she wanted to continue her search for Frank Lawton's killer, she quickly gave up any hope of stealing away from the planned activities. After the reception was over, everyone gathered in the gymnasium for dancing. As a member of the committee hosting the event, she was expected to actively participate.

Hazel was in bed when Delia returned to the house much later. Delia sat alone with a cup of tea thinking about her next step in the case. Based on the gossip she heard all through the night, the police were certain that Arch was the killer. She knew she needed to do something or the man would be convicted for defending the honor of her cousin.

CHAPTER TWENTY-THREE

Delia dressed quickly in the morning. The house was silent as she left her room but a smell from the kitchen told her that her cousin was awake. She found Hazel standing in front of the range.

"Good morning." Delia crossed over to the kitchen cabinet to get a teacup before joining Hazel at the range. "Did something burn?"

Hazel was staring at the pan in front of her.

Delia quickly set her teacup down and grabbed a towel. She used it to lift the scorched pan of eggs in front of Hazel. After setting it into the white porcelain sink, she turned on the faucet. The water spattered with a hissing noise as steam rose.

"Hazel, turn off the flame." When her cousin didn't respond, she nudged her out of the way and turned the knob herself.

"Come and sit." She held onto Hazel's arms and propelled her to the kitchen table. After gently pushing her down into the chair, she returned to get them both a cup of tea.

Hazel's face was covered with her hands when Delia set the teacup in front of her.

"Are you alright?" Delia took the seat next to her.

Hazel's hands dropped to the teacup. She wrapped them around the cup as though seeking the heat for comfort.

"This time last week I was frantic about the man-power bill." Hazel stared at her tea.

Delia's eyes fell to the newspaper on the table. One section was spread flat showing a full-page story about the upcoming registration date. Whereas before, those between twenty-one and thirty were required to register for the draft, the ages now were extended at both ends.

Men everywhere from eighteen to forty-five will be required to register on the same day. Multiple locations were opening up all over Glennon and every other town across the nation to process them all. Every possible location large enough to accommodate the numbers including churches, blacksmith shops, barbers, schoolhouses, and everything in between would be pressed into service.

Memories of Delia's own registration flashed through her mind. Like the men, she also was required to be physically examined after standing in a long line waiting for her turn. For some female yeomen, the experience proved a harrowing event. Others, like Delia, were permitted to wear a loose-fitting dress and a Navy nurse was present with the overworked physician who dispensed of his duties quickly before calling for the next recruit.

"He may still need to do so," Delia reminded her.

"If he's released from jail?" Hazel's eyes remained focused on her tea. "I know that. He'll make a fine soldier. He's very brave, you know. I keep telling myself that I'll be just as brave as he is when he goes. But this."

Delia knew what Hazel meant. Being accused of murder was different.

"I should make breakfast," Hazel said without moving.

"Perhaps I should take over that chore this morning," Delia suggested as she stood. "I'll clean the frying pan first."

"I'm not very hungry." Hazel's voice sounded far away.

"You need to keep your strength up. You don't want to get one of your headaches." Delia cut some of the crust from the bread to scrub the pan. When it didn't come completely clean, she dipped the crust into salt and tried again. "Are you planning to go to church this morning?"

"I don't feel up to it."

Delia reached for the washing soda. After putting some into the pan, she added hot water. "If rest will help stave off a headache, perhaps it is for the best that you remain here."

"You'll try to learn more today about Arch, won't you?"

Delia rinsed the pan and wiped it. She knew the police would be making their intentions known soon. She was running out of time. "I promise I'll do what I can."

***

After most of the congregation had emptied the church, Delia followed Mena past the pews and paused at the entrance to speak with her.

"How is Hazel holding up?" Mena asked quietly.

"As you might suspect." Delia nodded a greeting at a couple that passed them before following them outside.

Faye broke away from another cluster of people and joined them in front of the church. "Did you see the new principal and his sister?"

Delia glanced toward the street where Wesley Glennon stood

next to his sister as they spoke to a group of people around them. Her two children waited patiently beside them. At one point, Virginia Gray reached for her brother's arm. The little girl reached her hand up to take her uncle's other arm, just as her mother had but she wasn't tall enough. Her uncle reached down to hold the child's hand before saying something to make her laugh. Delia couldn't help smiling at the sight.

"How adorable," Mena murmured.

"I heard he was good with children," Faye whispered.

"The students at the normal school have spoken well of him also," Mena whispered back. "Such a shame his wife died in childbirth."

Faye turned to face them with her back against the street. "Earl Gordon told me last night that the new principal is very supportive of the commercial department."

"It sounds like he is fitting into the school community nicely," Mena said.

Delia assumed he must reserve his ill temper solely for her.

"I love your jacket Delia." Mabelle Neff touched the fabric as she stopped next to the others. "Very nice."

"Thank you." Delia opted not to explain that it used to belong to Euphemia. The admiral's wife had often gifted clothing she no longer wore to Delia. "Have any of you seen Carl Lawton?"

She watched the others exchange confused looks at her turn of conversation.

"I have not," Mena said.

"Perhaps he has been busy with his father's death?" Faye suggested.

Mena leaned in closer. "I imagine Mrs. Lawton has mixed feelings at the moment."

Mabelle nodded knowingly. "My mother heard that mister and missus were having more troubles than usual of late."

Their attention was drawn to the doorway as some of the students came out laughing. Delia waved to the ones she recognized hoping to get their attention.

Claude crossed over to join them. "Hello, all. What did you think?"

"Your singing was uplifting." Delia smiled to include the two young girls that followed Claude.

"We need to get back to the school," Gladys said as she tugged at Claude's sleeve.

"A group of us are planning a walk in the woods later," Rose explained. "For educational purposes, of course."

"Perhaps I should join you," Mabelle said. "You know that students aren't supposed to have unsupervised activities with boys and girls together."

"But…" Rose gave Gladys a helpless look.

"It wouldn't be a problem at all," Mabelle continued as she waved at the others. "And I may be able to add to the educational experience."

Delia watched them move off together lamenting the loss of the opportunity to ask about Carl. As they neared the street, the Glennon family finally began to walk away from the church.

"I just realized they weren't driving their motor car," Mena said. "I forgot about the ban for using gasoline on Sundays."

"I guess the shortages are touching all of us," Faye agreed.

CHAPTER TWENTY-FOUR

"And that concludes another day of typewriting." Delia turned to set her piece of chalk down. Behind her, she could hear the shuffling of feet as students rose to leave the classroom. Everyone began speaking at once as they gathered in clusters to walk out into the hallway. Delia turned back toward the students and moved to the other side of her desk.

"How was your educational walk in the woods yesterday?" she asked Gladys and Rose.

Gladys offered a rueful smile. "It was actually much better than I thought it would be."

"Miss Neff didn't assign any homework or give a surprise exam at the end," Rose agreed.

"I've been meaning to ask," Delia walked with them toward the door. "Have either of you heard anything about Carl Lawton?"

"I haven't," Gladys said as she stepped into the hall.

"I have." Rose stepped into the hall behind Gladys then

turned to face Delia. "Just yesterday, in fact. On our nature walk."

"Really?" Delia wasn't surprised given the boy's father had just died.

"One of my friends told me something." Rose's face wrinkled into thought as she tried to recall the specifics. "Edie said that she heard from Gussie who heard from Lizzy that someone saw him getting onto a train."

"A train? And did your friend's friend know when he may have gotten onto a train?"

Rose made another face. "I'm not sure. I know it was in the summer. I believe she may have said it was about a month or so ago."

"We should be going," Gladys said as she tugged on Rose's arm. "We need to meet Miss Neff in the sewing room."

"We help to make comfort clothing for the wounded soldiers," Rose explained.

"Wait," Delia said quickly. "Do you know where Claude is at this time of the day?"

The girls were walking backwards away from her. "He should be getting out of gymnasium class."

Delia waved before they turned and headed for the stairs. After collecting her hat, she followed them. The walk across campus was a pleasant one. As she drew closer to the gymnasium, she passed girls wearing black serge suits with sailor style blouses. They were all walking away from the gymnasium.

She picked up speed knowing that Claude would be exiting the two-story stone building and walking away from her toward the dormitories for men. She rounded the corner of the gymnasium in time to see him walk outside with a group of other young men.

Delia stood at the crosswalk waiting for him to come closer. When he saw her standing there watching him, he broke away from the other students.

"Miss Markham?"

"Claude, I'm sorry to trouble you but I just have a quick question." Delia stepped farther away from the group of young men.

Claude followed her. "Yes?"

She stopped and turned toward him. "Have you heard from Carl Lawton recently?"

The confusion left his face. "Oh yes, miss. Just this morning, in fact."

Delia tried not to show her excitement. "Claude, I know this sounds odd but I need to know what he told you."

The furrow between his brows reappeared. "Just that he had to go away, miss."

"He didn't tell you where he went?" She watched Claude shake his head. "Or why he left?"

"No, miss. He just asked me to watch after his mother." Claude lifted his hand when one of the others called his name. "I have to go."

"Oh, yes. Of course." Delia remained where she was. "Claude."

He paused to turn back toward her.

She knew he was eager to go with his friends. "If you hear from him again, you will tell me?"

His words were lost among the voices of his friends as they called to him again but she saw him nod his agreement. When he jogged over to his friends to catch up with them, Delia turned and walked in the other direction. It took several moments to get to the Biltmore Building. Delia climbed the steps to the second floor and found Bennie in his office.

"Miss Markham." Bennie stood from his desk.

She glanced at the principal's closed door.

"He isn't in at the moment," Bennie said. "He's at another meeting about the new military training program. Our unit will also be training officers. He seems pretty excited about that."

She ignored the relief she felt. "I'm not here to see him this time."

Bennie looked curious. "Is there something I can do to help you?"

"I was hoping I might use your telephone." Delia added a smile to her request.

Several minutes later, she left the Biltmore Building and headed for the hospital. It was a large building that doubled as an infirmary to handle most of the medical needs of hundreds of resident students. She found the nurse in her office at the front of the building.

Delia tapped on the door. "Nurse Noble?"

"Delia, hello. Please call me Blanche."

Delia stepped into the office. "Might I take up a few moments of your time?"

"Of course." Blanche set her pencil down and rested her clasped hands on her desk. "Is this about your injury?"

Delia saw the professional curiosity in Blanche's eyes. "Thank you, no. I was very nearly healed before I came to Hazel's. I do not anticipate any further issues with it."

"Then I will admit you have my interest. How can a nurse help a typewriting teacher?" Blanche's smile was contagious.

Delia felt herself smiling back. "I am hoping you can tell me about the effects of arsenate of lead."

Understanding flooded Blanche's eyes. "I see. How is Hazel

holding up?"

Once again, Delia wondered how much of a secret her cousin's relationship was.

"It has been very trying," Delia said. "Can you explain what might happen if someone ingested it?"

"Well." Blanche separated her hands. "It would depend on how much was administered."

"You're talking about the amount of poison given," Delia said.

"Yes. For example, if a very large amount was given the reaction would be somewhat different than smaller amounts over a long period."

"How so?"

"With a large amount, the patient might suffer from severe stomach cramps, diarrhea, convulsions, and vomiting."

"Would death occur immediately with a large amount?" Delia asked.

Blanche made a face as she considered the possibilities. "Again, it would depend on just how much he was given. It is possible it wouldn't be instantaneous."

"I understand that Arch believed he wasn't missing a large amount. In fact, he doesn't believe he was missing any at all. It's the police who are trying to prove otherwise. What if the victim was given small amounts over time?"

"The poison would have impacted his body but more slowly. The symptoms would have been there but would be less obvious," Blanche said.

"Can you give examples?"

"He may have suffered from poor appetite. Perhaps he felt weak or tired."

"Those are things that may not have been noticeable at first," Delia murmured.

"Exactly. He might attribute them to any number of things. Perhaps he'd been working too hard lately, that sort of thing," Blanche said.

"What might happen if he was given poison for an extended period and then the poison was stopped?"

Blanche looked surprised at first, but her face turned thoughtful as she considered the implications. She shook her head slowly. "The poison would have taken its toll. The chances are good that his organs would have failed. It was only a matter of time."

CHAPTER
TWENTY-FIVE

Delia left the hospital preoccupied in thought. Without intent, she walked along the many paved paths that crossed the campus. She paused in front of the library and considered stopping in to see Mena for a moment. As she debated the idea, a large group of students passed by her on their way to the library entrance all talking at once.

She turned away and continued walking as she reviewed the things she had learned. She was convinced that Arch Keaton had not killed Frank Lawton. Though she knew his proximity to the poison gave him the means, the image of his character sketched by the many people of Glennon who knew him argued his innocence.

He was a man who gave willingly of his time to the instruction of Sam. Indeed, his guidance would be considered paternal by many. He was a man of honor who would fight to shield Hazel from the ugliness of the world. He was a man who tenderly nurtured acres of plants and trees then carefully harvested them in support of the many who partook of the bounty.

On the other hand, Frank Lawton's former partner was quite the opposite. Bob Hinkle's character was found lacking in every possible regard. His own wife considered his potential for murder nonexistent due to the amount of effort it would require.

She was certain the killer wasn't Arch. She was fairly certain it wasn't Bob Hinkle. Her investigation of those two men had led her to believe they did not hold the answers she needed. Whereas, in contrast, the victim's family left many unanswered questions.

She was standing near a beautiful display of Culver's root, asters, and golden sneezeweed lost in thought when Bennie found her.

"Miss Markham!" Bennie was out of breath when he stopped next to her. "You have a telegram."

She held her hand out to take the missive. Euphemia must have acted with great haste after Delia's earlier telephone call to produce such a speedy result from the admiral's office.

"I couldn't help but know the contents," Bennie said.

"Quite alright," she murmured as she finished reading. "This will do nicely."

"Would you like me to accompany you?" Bennie asked.

She smiled her thanks. "That won't be necessary. I am acquainted with such offices."

A short time later, she was taking the now familiar trip on the trolley from the front of Glennon Normal School to downtown Glennon. Along the way, they ran parallel to a sidewalk that led all the way from the school campus into downtown Glennon. As the trolley moved deeper into the town, there were many more paved sidewalks lined with electric street lamps along the main streets for pedestrians.

She watched as they passed an ice wagon. Although the horse steadily pulled the yellow wagon with red wheels over the brick-paved street it was no match for the speed of the trolley. When the trolley turned a corner it had to slow to avoid a motor car passing in front of it. Finally, they made it to her stop.

According to the newspaper, the primary recruiting office in Glennon was shifting its location in anticipation of the large influx of men required to report for the next draft registration. The new location was located on the second floor of the Glennon Bank.

Delia stepped inside the large building occupying the corner of Main Street and West Second and looked for signs that directed her to the stairs. Noises from above could be heard as she gathered her skirts and began ascending. When she reached the second floor, she stood in an open space and watched the activity.

There were several men everywhere trying to devise separate workspaces from the large area. Most of them ignored her. One gentleman paused in his work and fixed her with a stare. Delia saw a frown cross his face as she approached him.

"This area is a recruiting office." He was perhaps in his fifties and was without a jacket. His shirt sleeves were rolled up due to his exertion and the heat on the second floor.

Behind him, men continued about their duties setting up chairs, desks, and tables. One man in the far corner stopped what he was doing and walked toward them.

"I would like to ask you some questions," Delia said.

The first man didn't attempt to hide his scowl as the second one approached from behind him.

"What's this?" the second one asked.

"Another one of those suffragettes, I'll wager." The first man began to turn away.

"Sir, if I may." Delia held out the telegram. "This is from Admiral Hobart Jennings of the United States Navy."

Both men stared at her. Finally, curiosity won out. The first man reached for it. The second one read over his shoulder.

"I'll be."

"As you see from the message, my name is Miss Delia Markham. And you are?"

The second man answered. "I'm Ray, miss. This here is Paul."

Paul held up the telegram. "How is it you know an admiral in the Navy?"

"I served under him." Delia nodded at the telegram. "What can you tell me?"

"You have to understand, we process a lot of men." Paul frowned at the paper in his hand.

Ray tapped his arm. "We have the records in the boxes." He pointed behind them. "I was just starting to work on them."

"We're in the process of moving from a smaller location," Paul said as Ray walked away.

"Understandable. I'm sure you'll have things in order in no time." Delia watched as Ray walked back toward them holding a file.

"Here it is. Carl Lawton, age twenty." Ray looked up from the folder. "He volunteered just in time. If he had waited any longer, he wouldn't have been allowed."

Delia nodded her understanding. Once the age for the draft was lowered to eighteen, volunteering was no longer an option. The men would now be draftees and had to wait to be called to duty.

"How long ago did he volunteer?" Delia asked.

"Been about six weeks now. He's probably on his way over to the fighting." Ray closed the folder in his hand.

Delia left the bank building and walked to the Electric Shoe

Repair. She wasn't surprised to find Sadie Lawton hard at work. This time when Delia entered the shop, Sadie's eyes filled with fear. The buzzing of the sewing machine stopped. Sadie remained where she was, staring at Delia.

Delia closed the distance between them and gentled her voice. "I know that he was trying to protect you." She watched as Sadie's eyes closed. "You may not know this but he sent a letter to one of my students. Carl asked Claude to look after you while he's gone."

A tear worked its way from Sadie's eye but she remained quiet as Delia continued.

"Sadie, I know he joined the service. I just received confirmation from the recruitment office."

More tears joined the first as Sadie began crying in earnest. Delia reached for her handkerchief. She put one hand on Sadie's shoulder and pressed the handkerchief into Sadie's hand with the other.

"Sadie, an innocent man is about to be convicted. Only you can help him," Delia said.

Sadie pressed the handkerchief against her eyes. "Carl was only trying to protect me. He's a good boy. He couldn't stand by and watch his father treat me like that anymore."

"Carl began to poison him with the arsenate of lead," Delia said. It wasn't a question.

Sadie nodded as another sob broke free.

Delia needed to know. "Did he take the poison from the school?"

Sadie's head came up. "Carl is not a thief." Her eyes flashed with indignation. "Arsenate of lead is sold everywhere. He bought it himself. I can prove it. He wrote a letter confessing everything and left it with me." Fresh tears threatened to spill over. "He said it was in case the police suspected me."

CHAPTER
TWENTY-SIX

"I'm sorry. Though I am familiar with many in Glennon, I have never had the occasion to socialize with any of the members of the police." Mena removed her spectacles and began cleaning them with a daintily embroidered linen handkerchief.

Delia felt her hopes sink. She stood on the other side of the front desk and watched Mena situate the gold-filled frames with riding bow temples to their proper position. Delia looked down at the letter she clutched in her hand.

"Why are you asking me about the police?" Mena's eyes dropped to the letter.

"I have to do something." Delia took a step away from the front desk.

"You aren't planning to go to the police station alone, are you?" Mena sounded slightly alarmed.

"I believe I shall have to. I hold the evidence in my hands to free Mr. Keaton," Delia said as she turned to leave.

"Wait!" Mena's eyes widened at the volume of her own voice.

She quickly came around the front desk to reach Delia. "Have Principal Glennon go."

"What? Why him?"

"He knows the chief of police." Mena put her hand on Delia's arm. "It is the perfect solution. The captain is technically responsible for the employees here. It makes sense."

Though the thought of yet another combative encounter with the captain was less than appealing, Delia couldn't argue with Mena's logic.

"Very well. I will go to him directly." She patted Mena's hand. "You are correct. Both his position and his connections should hold more sway. Thank you."

Delia walked quickly across the campus to the Biltmore Building. This time when she reached Bennie's office, her eyes went straight to the principal's door.

"Miss Markham." Bennie stood from his desk and came around to join her. "Is anything the matter?"

Delia held up the letter. "Is he in?"

Bennie glanced at the paper in her hand before crossing over to the closed door. After he slipped into the principal's office, Delia heard muffled voices on the other side.

When Bennie emerged, he left the door open. "Principal Glennon will see you now."

Delia smiled her thanks before crossing over to the door. After stepping inside, she stood in front of the principal's desk and waited for him to acknowledge her presence.

He finished reading the paper on his desk then reached for his pen. After signing his name, he looked up. "To what do I owe this pleasure?"

Delia thought he looked anything but pleased. She stepped forward and set the letter from Carl Lawton on the desk. She continued standing while he read. When he was done, he pushed it away.

"Well?"

He looked mildly confused. "Well, what?"

She managed to control her impatience just in time. "I thought perhaps you might consider appealing to the police on behalf of Mr. Keaton to set him free."

"You believe the letter offers substantial evidence to acquit him of the crime with which he has been charged?"

She didn't try to hide the disbelief from her face. "You do not?"

"Oh, I imagine the chief of police will find it of interest." His gaze held hers.

Delia saw the amusement in his eyes. "You mock me."

"Only insomuch that your presence here now surprises me," he said.

"In what way?"

He motioned toward the letter. "You have found the murderer. I dare not ask what methods you employed to succeed."

"Does it matter? The end result is the same. Arch Keaton can be set free."

"I only wonder why you did not storm the police station yourself to demand the man's release."

She crossed her arms. "I considered it."

"Yet here you are," he pointed out.

"I was persuaded to believe that given your role here..." She stopped when he laughed. It was an unexpected sound.

"No doubt the Navy regretted its decision allowing you to enlist before the ink on your papers were dry." He pressed his fingers into his eyes briefly before dropping his hand. "I hope this means you will apply your full attention to your duties as a teacher from this point forward."

His words stung but she still saw amusement in his eyes when he spoke. Delia stepped forward and reached for Carl's letter of confession.

Wes placed his hand firmly over the paper. "I believe I can take it from here, Yeoman Markham."

Delia felt her chin go up. "I should not wish to trouble you in any way, Captain."

He lifted the paper and waved it. "You are dismissed."

She considered continuing her argument but decided that she had succeeded with her mission. At least, she hoped she had. "You will take the letter to the police?"

"Yes, yes." He looked past her toward the door.

She turned and saw Bennie standing there. He stepped away from the door to allow her to pass by. She didn't miss the grin on his face before he closed the door behind them.

"Good job," he whispered.

With one last look at the door, she smiled as she walked away.

***

"You know you're very nearly out of the poultice he made up," Otis said.

"I am sure I will survive." Wes began unknotting his tie as he crossed through his private suite in Glennon House.

"Yes, but I may not. I have had much better use of my arm since applying it," Otis said loudly so Wes could hear him in the other room.

Wes appeared in the doorway with his tie hanging loosely around his neck. He looked longingly at the crystal decanter.

"You would deny me a glass of Pennsylvania rye after working all day?"

"Not at all. I'll be happy to pour it for you." Otis crossed over to Wes and reached for his tie. "When you return from the police station."

"If I have to go, you're coming with me," Wes grumbled as Otis fumbled with his tie.

Otis perked up. "I'll drive."

"With your arm? Hardly." Wes batted Otis's good arm away. "I haven't seen Judson Heath in years."

"You were friends with him?" Otis followed Wes toward the door.

"More like competitors." Wes cinched his tie as he went out into the hall. "I'm not sure he's ever forgiven me for the time I stole home in a baseball game."

"You made the winning point?" Otis stepped into the elevator.

"I knocked him over as I slid across the base," Wes said as he watched Otis work the controls. "He broke his leg in the process."

Otis winced. "Tell me he's forgiven you."

"Doubtful." Wes said. "It never did heal properly. He's had a limp ever since."

Otis stepped out into the main floor hallway first. "Do not tell me the story gets worse."

"I'm guessing it's what kept him out of the war," Wes said as he followed Otis from the house.

"Perhaps he's gotten over it," Otis said hopefully.

Thirty minutes later they sat in the police station waiting for Judson Heath. When a dark-haired man finally emerged from his office and limped across the room toward them, he neither smiled nor held out his hand to greet Wes.

Wes stood and held out his hand. "Judson. Good to see you."

Judson glared at him for a long moment before clasping Wes's hand. "I heard you were back. One of my men told me you were here to see the prisoner after he was first brought in."

Wes motioned toward Otis who had also risen to stand next to him. "Otis Hart."

Judson's eyes shifted from Wes to Otis. He gave a brief nod then returned his focus to Wes. "I don't imagine this is a social call."

"We're here about Arch Keaton," Wes said.

"We have all the evidence we need to convict him. Thanks for stopping by." Judson turned to walk away.

Wes moved to intercept him. "Judson, please. Hear me out. A man's innocence hangs in the balance."

"He had access to the arsenate of lead," Judson said.

"Along with everyone else," Wes agreed.

"Witnesses saw him arguing with the victim shortly before he died," Judson said stubbornly.

"As we have argued over your failure to move away from home base?" Wes watched Judson debate his response. Just as he was sure the man was ready to walk away, Otis spoke.

"We have a signed confession from the real killer," Otis said quietly. "Surely it's worth your time to read it?"

Judson shifted his focus from Otis to Wes. "Why didn't you say so?"

Wes reached for the letter in his pocket. "I wanted to make sure you would read it and not destroy it."

Judson snatched it from Wes's hand. He shook his head when

he was done and walked away.

"Stay here," he called back to them.

Otis started to follow Judson.

Wes stopped him. "Wait."

"That is the only copy of the letter," Otis pointed out.

"Judson may be angry at me but he isn't a bad man," Wes said quietly.

A moment later, Arch appeared with Judson behind him. Arch held Carl's letter in his hand.

"We need to decide what we're going to do about this," Judson said.

"He confessed to killing his father," Otis said.

"Yes, but he is now in the war fighting for our side," Arch argued.

"I should think you'd be eager to have him brought back here to stand trial," Wes said. "You were nearly convicted for a crime you didn't commit."

Arch shook his head. "Leave him be. If he makes it back from the war, you can deal with it then."

Judson started to argue.

Arch held up his hand. "You didn't know the boy's father as I did. He most certainly was abusing his wife. No doubt he also took his anger out on the son. I'm sure Carl was only trying to protect his mother. Frank had her working her fingers to the bone at that repair shop nonstop day in and day out."

Judson lifted his brows at Wes.

Wes nodded once and put his hand on Arch's shoulder. "Let's get out of here. There's a decanter of Pennsylvania rye wondering where I've been."

CHAPTER TWENTY-SEVEN

He winced as the fingers seemed to bury themselves deep into the wound in his back. "You would think as often as you've done this you could accomplish it more quickly."

"If you would bother to remain still, it wouldn't take as long," Otis said as he applied more of the poultice.

"Tell that to the fiend who shot me," Wes snarled as Otis pushed against a particularly painful area.

"I do believe this new batch smells even worse than the last." Otis dipped his fingers into the bottle before gently dabbing more poultice on Wes's wound.

Wes clenched his teeth as another searing stab of pain radiated through him. "I hope his place in Hades does not have to be held long."

Otis set the bottle down and reached for a bandage. "If only I had seen him at the time. I would have shortened the wait."

It was a subject they had discussed many times.

"We were on the battlefield. It was chaos," Wes ground out.

"Any fiend that would shoot another man in the back." Otis let the sentence hang as he finished with the bandage.

Wes felt the pain begin to ease by small degrees. "As I recall, you had your own problems to deal with."

Otis sank his fingers into the poultice and began applying it to his shoulder. "I only hope that one or both of us are there to see the man is given his just due."

"We are no closer to finding the identity of the fiend now than we were at the time he shot us." Wes tried to unclench his jaw. "More to the point, the Army still believes I was running away from the fight when it happened."

"I am your witness," Otis protested.

"You were wounded at the same time. They determined that there was a margin of error in your assessment of the situation given the ordeal of your own injury." Wes reached for his shirt. "While I appreciate your loyalty in defending my honor, I do not wish you to suffer my fate along with me."

"I know what I know," Otis argued. "It is what I keep repeating to them."

"Let us hope it is enough for now." Wes gingerly tried to slide an arm into a sleeve.

"Long enough for us to find the identity of the fiend who shot us." Otis pressed a bandage over the poultice on his shoulder.

Wes managed to get his other arm into the sleeve. He turned to face Otis and saw him fumbling with the bandage.

"Here then." Wes attempted to secure the dressing.

Otis batted his hands away. "With your abilities for healing, I'll see Hades before the fiend."

Wes gave up and crossed over to his chair. After sinking into it, he lifted his cup of coffee. What little was left was already cold. "At least the specifics about my injury have been kept from the general populace, thanks to you. If you hadn't been there to argue that I wasn't retreating in the face of enemy fire, I would have been the first to reach the infernal region."

"Let us hope the Army allows it to remain that way," Otis said pointedly. "We do not wish to have them telling any version of the story until we can flush out the fiend ourselves."

"Have you learned anything from your contacts in Washington?" Wes pushed himself up from the chair.

"Nothing." The frustration in his voice was obvious. "It's as though the fiend were some sort of specter. He appeared from nowhere to shoot us down then was gone just as quickly."

"More like a demon," Wes muttered as he poured two cups of coffee.

"By why take aim at us?" It wasn't the first time Otis had asked the question.

"I told you, old man. The only thing that makes sense is that the fiend was after me." Wes handed a cup of coffee to Otis before retaking his seat. He watched Otis lower himself into another chair carefully to avoid spilling his coffee. "You merely happened to be in the way."

"Perhaps," Otis agreed. "But the fiend made a mistake when he did so. He gained another enemy."

Wes let out a breath. "I would understand completely if you left this fight to me."

"So you have said many times before. We have a better chance of discovering the fiend if we work together. For now, you must continue to suffer through my poor imitation of a gentleman's gentleman."

The tapping at the door interrupted Wes's response.

"Come," Wes said loudly then watched as the door swung open.

Bennie stood in the doorway. "Good morning."

Wes saw the paper in his hands. "A message this early in the morning?"

"Telegram, sir."

"Let's have it then." Wes held his hand out.

Bennie remained where he was. "It isn't addressed to you, sir. It's for Miss Markham."

"Indeed." Wes eyed the paper with interest. "So you are here instead?"

"Technically, I should not allow anyone else to see the message," Bennie said as he took a few steps into the room.

Wes shifted his eyes to Otis.

"But you couldn't help knowing the contents yourself," Otis said. "Perhaps it is something the captain should be aware of? Something that involves the school?"

Bennie hesitated for only a moment before reading the telegram. When he was done, he looked back up at Wes. "I am certain the whole town will know soon, sir."

Wes steepled his hands together as he considered the news. "Thank you, Bennie. Miss Markham should be getting out of her first class soon."

Bennie stepped backwards toward the door. "Yes, sir. I'll take it over to Glennon Hall now."

"And Bennie?"

"Yes, Captain?" Bennie stopped in the doorway.

"The other two boys. The ones who were stealing the food. How have they been working out?" Wes asked.

"I'm told the kitchen steward has kept them busy working off the food they took from the school, sir." Bennie reached for the door handle. "Between their classes and the work schedule they've been assigned, they no longer have the free time for late-night activities."

***

Delia pressed the button on the stop watch. "And that's it. Time is up and class is over. I'll see you all when we meet again."

Delia opened the drawer of her desk and set her watch inside as the students began gathering their things to leave.

"I managed to finish all of the words that time," Rose said as she followed Gladys from the room.

"I think I may have made one mistake in mine." Gladys paused at the door to wave to Delia.

"Perhaps you'll manage a perfect attempt next time," Delia said as she watched the girls leave the room.

Once all of the students were gone, she sat down at her desk in the silence of the room. After opening another drawer, she pulled out a few sheets of writing paper and a pen.

"Miss Markham?" Bennie stood at the open door.

"Yes, Bennie?" Delia set her pen down.

"You have a telegram." Bennie crossed over to the front of her desk and held it out.

Delia took the paper and unfolded it. Her hand went to her mouth as she read it. "That is so sad."

"Yes, miss."

Delia looked up. "Do you think his mother knows yet?"

"Probably, miss. The Army is very good about such things."

Delia closed her eyes for a moment as she thought about Sadie Lawton. The woman was all alone now. Both her husband and her son were gone.

"Pneumonia." Delia shook her head. "I can't believe Carl died on the ship from an illness going over to the fighting. He never even made it to the war."

"At least he'll be sent back here for burial." Bennie turned to leave. "His mother will have that much."

"Thank you, Bennie. Does the captain know?"

Bennie stopped at the door and turned a guilty face toward Delia. "Yes, miss. I thought he should know seeing as it involved the school."

"Of course." Delia offered an understanding smile just before Bennie disappeared from view. When she was alone again, she reached for her pen to write to the admiral's wife.

Dearest Euphemia. I am now settling into my new position here at Glennon Normal School. I have yet to learn anything about our mutual friend but have had occasion to speak with him more than once. I will continue to monitor the situation as requested and will report back promptly with any news. With fondest regards, Delia.

FURTHER READING

Information about women serving in World War I in the United States can be found from the Navy's website and elsewhere online. There are also books on the topic specific to Yeoman (f). Two examples are below.

Butler, H. F. (1967). I was a yeoman (F). Washington, D.C.: Naval Historical Foundation.

Ebbert, J. and Hall, M.-B. (2002). The first, the few, the forgotten: Navy and Marine Corps women in World War I. Annapolis, Md: Naval Institute Press.

COMING SOON

Coming soon: The next book in the Glennon Normal School Historical Mystery series.

Glennon Normal School Historical Mystery Series
Early September 1918. The Great War. Although the world is at war, Delia Markham is adjusting to her job as a typewriting teacher at Glennon Normal School in the fall term of 1918. Her new life revolves around teaching future teachers. It isn't an easy transition from her former assignment as Yeoman (F) in the U. S. Naval Reserve. When circumstances involve her in a mystery, some of the past excitement finds its way back into her life.

Made in the USA
Columbia, SC
07 April 2021